Home

WISHING FOR A HOME

T.A. CHASE

Wishing for a Home
ISBN # 978-1-78184-589-9
©Copyright T.A. Chase 2013
Cover Art by Posh Gosh ©Copyright February 2013
Interior text design by Claire Siemaszkiewicz
Total-E-Bound Publishing

Published in 2013 by Total-E-Bound Publishing, Think Tank, Ruston Way, Lincoln, LN6 7FL, United Kingdom.

.

WISHING FOR A HOME

Dedication

The men in my Home series have become like friends to me and to all my readers. Thank you for falling in love with them, and for pushing me to give all of them their own happy endings.

Prologue

Derek St Martin fell on the bed, burying his face in his pillow. It had been eight months since he'd slept in his own bed and he was ready for a vacation. The tour had been rough. His body hurt and his voice had deserted him before the last gig. Somehow he'd managed to suck it up and give a great show.

His head pounded. Shit. He rolled over, contemplating how much energy it would take to go and grab some pills from the bathroom. More than he had at the moment.

Closing his eyes, he tried to relax. The pounding stopped for a moment and he sighed. When the noise started again, Derek realised someone was knocking on his front door.

"Fuck," he muttered, ignoring whoever it was.

He really wasn't in any shape to talk to people. After sitting up, he tugged his T-shirt over his head and tossed it on the floor. He flopped back to his bed, covering his eyes with his arm.

"Hey, man, you okay?"

Derek almost levitated off the mattress when Eddie's voice sounded in the room. Frowning, he glanced under his arm to the doorway and saw his stepbrother, Edward Monterrose, leaning against the doorframe.

"Need sleep," he whispered, which was about all the volume he could achieve.

"I know. Let's get you comfortable."

He didn't protest as Eddie stripped him and threw a blanket over him.

"Do you need anything?"

"Pills. Bathroom. Little blue ones."

Derek listened to Eddie's footsteps as he moved from room to room. The medicine cabinet door shut and water ran.

"Here."

Eddie slipped an arm around his shoulder and propped him up enough to swallow the pills down with some water.

"Thanks."

He curled up around a pillow, pressed his face against the cool cotton fabric and waited for the meds to kick in.

"I'll be back in a few days. We need to talk about that pharmacy in your bathroom."

Derek didn't hear Eddie leave. He'd slipped into the easy floating where he didn't hurt and he wasn't lonely.

* * * *

At some point during the night, Derek swam out of the sleep fog he'd been in. He didn't check the clock, not caring what time it was, or even how long he'd slept. His body still ached and his head still pounded, so obviously he hadn't been under long enough.

He stumbled to the bathroom, took a piss, and ignored his reflection in the mirror as he washed his hands. Derek searched through the bottles scattered all over the bathroom counter, looking for the one with the sleeping pills in them. Christ, if he didn't have any more Ambien, he was going to flip out. He knew he should have filled the prescription before he headed home, but all he could think about was his bed.

Holding a couple of the bottles up, he squinted, struggling to read the words written on the labels. None of them made any sense, running together in black blocks. Derek threw them down and shuffled out, knowing he probably had some whisky somewhere. He'd figured out some time ago that if he didn't have any pills, at least liquor would put him to sleep.

At the moment, he wasn't picky about what kind of alcohol, as long as it worked. He needed another twenty-four hours of sleep or so to even begin to feel normal. Not bothering to turn on any lights, he made his way into the living room, and found the bar. He held tight to the bottle he'd grabbed, trying to open the cap with trembling hands. Just as he was going to throw a fit and chuck the liquor across the room, he got the cap off, and took two big swigs.

The burning sensation eased off into a burst of warmth in his stomach, causing his tense muscles to relax. Keeping a tight grip on the bottle, he snatched a blanket off the back of the couch as he passed it on the way to the balcony. Somehow, he got the sliding glass door open without falling face first through it, or dropping any of the items he carried.

He stumbled over the edge of the blanket, flailed wildly, and landed with a thud in the lounge chair he'd been heading for anyway. Derek set the bottle on the ground next to him, then wiggled around until he was covered with the blanket. He closed his eyes and sighed.

For most of his life, he'd heard music in his head, and it filtered over into his dreams, but in the last eight months—longer than that, actually—everything had been ominously silent. It was like his life had got so fucked up, even his music had deserted him. The crickets and other night animals filled the dark up with noise, and even that would help soothe him enough to sleep some more.

As Derek drifted along on the buzz from the alcohol, he wondered if there was a place he could just *be* for a while. Not worry about being Derek St fucking Martin and the world's hottest country singer. A place where he could be a guy who liked other guys, and maybe even kissed one once in a while. He rolled his eyes.

"Listen to my pity party. Shit. I sound pathetic," he muttered into the night air. "You'd think I was homeless and had no friends. I've got everything I could want, and I knew what I signed on for when I agreed to this shit."

Yet after eight years, he was thinking it might not have been worth it. Selling his soul and the very truth of who he was for money and fame. Derek took another sip from the bottle before he shoved all those depressing thoughts out of his mind. He'd be in a better mood when he could think clearly.

Chapter One

Nashville, Tennessee
Two days later

Derek curled up in his favourite recliner, a glass dangling from his fingers. He rested his head against the cushion and closed his eyes.

"Derek, you need to get away."

He didn't look at Eddie, who had respected his need to sleep and waited two days before coming back. Except for getting up to take more pills, pee, and drink some more alcohol, he hadn't even tried to act like a normal human being until this morning.

"I'd love to, but there isn't anywhere I can go where I won't be recognised." He opened one eye and checked out where Eddie stood.

One wall of his living room was made entirely of windows, giving him an unobstructed view of the lake. He often sat and watched the deer come down to drink at night. His brother stood there now, staring out of the window.

"If I found you a place, would you go?" He turned and Derek saw the worry in his eyes.

Derek shrugged, then took a sip of whisky and closed his eyes. "Not sure a place like that exists."

"Sounds fucking arrogant, Derek." Eddie sat down on the couch and leant forward, resting his elbows on his knees.

"I know it does, but it's the truth. Don't you think I've tried to get away? Do you think I like having to be Derek St fucking Martin all the time?" He swallowed the rest of his whisky.

He pushed to his feet and staggered to the bar where a half-empty bottle sat. Setting his glass on the counter, he started to pour another drink.

"No more."

Eddie took the bottle and glass away. Derek braced his arms against the smooth wooden edge. His throat still hurt, but the pounding in his head had lessened slightly.

"Fine." He'd wait until he was alone again.

"You need to stop this shit, Derek. The booze and pills aren't good for you." Eddie sat on the stool next to him and shook his head. "I can't believe Thomas lets you do this."

Derek laughed harshly. "The pills keep me going. I can rest with the sleeping pills. Other pills for energy so I can perform. The alcohol dulls it all so I don't care how fucking messed up everything's gotten."

He went back to the chair, drawing his knees under his chin and wrapping his arms around them.

"Thomas could care less as long as I can sing, continue to make him obscene amounts of money, and don't get caught fucking a guy."

Eddie poured himself a drink. "You chose this life. You don't have to go to all those parties and clubs. It's your choice to drink and pop pills. I thought country singers weren't quite as caught up in the whole scene as rock stars."

Snorting, Derek eyed his brother. "You're kidding, right? Haven't you ever heard of any of those country singers whose careers were cut short because of all the boozing and hard living they did? I'm just following in illustrious footsteps, my friend."

"But I thought this is what you wanted." Eddie gestured to include the expensive furniture, the large house, and the gold records on the walls.

He sighed. "That's the twisted, fucked-up thing. When I started all this shit, I would have given anything to be successful. Eight years later, I'm starting to think I sold my soul."

Eddie sat on the coffee table in front of Derek and reached out, putting a hand on his knee. "Is all of this simply because you're gay and you have to pretend not to be?"

Laughing, he shook his head. "It's only a small part of a bigger problem, Eddie. When I first fell in love with music, all I could think about was the music, the lyrics, and the songs. Then I became famous and there isn't time to focus on the music anymore. I have to be seen and be 'on' all the time. I have to keep in shape because a fat singer doesn't sell records, unless he's Elvis, and I've never claimed to have that kind of talent. I have to smile and look like I'm enjoying my life."

"I feel for you, man. It must be terrible having all this and having to act like you enjoy it." Eddie's voice dripped with sarcasm.

He slapped Eddie's hand off his knee and shot to his feet. Pacing from the windows to the bar, he shoved his hands through his hair and moaned. His head hurt and he longed to take another blue pill. Drifting along on whatever current he found sounded like a great way to spend his vacation, though if he didn't go somewhere, Thomas would find him and drag him out to do some sort of publicity thing.

Also, as much as he had come to depend on the liquor and drugs to soften the edges cutting his nerves to shreds, he knew the danger he was in. He didn't want to be a stereotypical drug-addicted musician. Shit, he simply wanted to play his guitar and sing.

He froze in front of the bar, staring at himself in the mirror above it. He'd been blessed with slightly golden skin, looking like he always had a tan. Dark circles had taken up permanent residence under his eyes and he realised he looked older than his thirty-two years. Hell, he felt older than thirty-two as well. He was so tired of everything, and he wasn't sure he could take much more of it.

Dropping his gaze to stare at the cream carpet under his bare feet, he hunched his shoulders and asked for help from the only person he trusted.

"Eddie, I need help."

"I know." Moving to his side, Eddie slipped his arm around his shoulders. "First, we have to get rid of the shit in your system. You're sliding quickly down a terrible slope, brother, and now that I know how bad it is, I refuse to let you go."

As his brother's words washed over him, Derek relaxed. A fresh pair of eyes and a person who didn't derive their living from Derek's talent was just what he needed to help him get a grip on his life.

"Thank you."

"We only have each other, Derek. You're the brother of my heart, even if we don't share any blood." Eddie hugged him quickly before stepping away to start pacing himself. "I might have a place for you to hang out. How long before you have to go back into the studio?"

Derek returned to the chair and allowed the soft cushions to swallow him. "Three months. Thomas and the record label weren't going to give me that much, but my doctor told them I was on the verge of a breakdown and needed to get away from the business for a while." He tilted his head and said, "I haven't written a damn thing since before this last tour. It's all gone silent in my head."

"Could be all the drugs," Eddie suggested.

"Nah. It never made a difference before." He rested his forehead on his knees and rocked. "There's a part of me ready to toss the whole thing and run away."

"Hmmm...let me make a call."

He pointed to the phone on the end table. "You can use that."

"Thanks, but I think I'll go in your study."

Shrugging, Derek waved Eddie away and started humming one of his hit songs.

* * * *

Edward flipped open his cell phone and scrolled through his numbers. Finding the right one, he pressed 'dial' and listened to it ring. He had to save Derek, the way his stepbrother had saved him, all those years ago when their families had been combined.

"Hello?"

"Les, it's Edward Monterrose."

"Edward, how are you? How's Gypsy working out for you?" the ex-show rider asked, referring to the horse he'd trained for Edward.

Les Hardin's voice was a welcome sound and Edward allowed relief to swamp him. Les had been a friend since they'd competed in the same horse shows. It was show jumping's loss when Les had to retire due to injury.

"Gypsy's doing great, Les. Working with you really straightened both of us out."

He rubbed his forehead and sat at Derek's oak desk. Staring around the room, he noticed how bare it was. Decorated by one of the city's top interior designers, the entire house, except Derek's bedroom, had a showcase look—as if no one lived there and it was only for display.

"You sound worried, Edward. How can I help you?"

God, if Les could hear his concern over the phone, he must not be handling Derek's problems as well as he thought.

"You remember my stepbrother, Derek?"

A rustling came over the phone, like Les was settling into a chair or something.

"Yes, I do. He's hit the big time now with his singing. Tell him congratulations when you see him next. I like his stuff."

"Well, he's the reason I'm calling. His last tour just ended and he's not doing so hot. In fact, the doctor forced his manager and record company to give him a vacation. He's strung out. I was wondering if I could send him out to your ranch for three months. I know you won't bother him and he can recover there. I can't watch over him because I have a ton of horse shows to compete in the next several months."

Something in the tone of Edward's voice must have alerted Les.

"There's another reason why you want him to come here. What makes my ranch the place for Derek?"

Edward gritted his teeth. He didn't want to break Derek's confidence, but he also trusted Les not to spill the secret to anyone.

"Derek's gay, Les. He needs a place where he knows he doesn't have to hide that part of himself. I'm not saying he'll turn into a flaming queen or anything, but if he has one less thing to hide, he might be able to relax enough to actually heal."

"Gay, huh?" Les chuckled. "I can hear female hearts breaking all over the country if word of that got out."

"And millions of happy gay boys will be over the moon at the thought of him playing for their team."

"True." Les was silent for a moment. "Let me see what I can do. Randy and I are taking off for a couple of weeks. Tony's nephew is competing in Germany and we're all heading over there to support him."

Disappointment rose in him. "I understand, Les. I'll try to figure somewhere else. If I don't send him somewhere no one can find him, they won't let him rest."

"Oh, I'm not saying he can't come. I just need to work the arrangements out. I'm not sure my ranch is the best place for him anyway. Too many people come and go here, but maybe Tony and Brody would be willing to let him stay at their place while we're all in Germany."

"I would appreciate anything you could do or even suggest to me, Les. I don't want to lose him. He's my only real family."

"Give me a few minutes and I'll call you back."

"I'll be waiting."

He hung up and set his phone on the desk. He didn't want to go and face Derek until he had a plan in place to help him. True to his words, Les called back a few minutes later.

"Brody said to send him out. Derek can use the main house and they'll have their foreman to keep an eye on him. No one will bother him, and hopefully the clean air of Wyoming will help clear his mind."

"Thanks. I owe you big."

"No, you don't. Friends help each other and I have a favour to ask of you. While you're at the shows, can you keep your eye out for a couple young horses? I'm looking to pick up a few more for Juan."

"I can do that. Thanks again."

"No problem. Call me with the flight plans and I'll be there to pick Derek up at the airport."

Edward hung up, feeling better about his brother's chances.

Derek had moved to the couch when Eddie returned to the living room and sat on the coffee table again. Staring at his brother, he wished Eddie would leave so he could get back to bed.

"Here's the deal. In two days, you're going to fly to Cheyenne, Wyoming. A friend of mine is going to meet you there."

He looked at Eddie in mock surprise. "You're sending me to ranch country. No one will recognise me there."

Eddie flipped him the finger. "You'll be staying at the RM ranch. Tony Romanos and Brody MacCafferty are friends of my friend and are willing to let you stay at their place."

"Brody MacCafferty?" He chuckled. "He used to do some bodyguard work for me."

"Good. Brody and Tony won't be there, but their foreman will be. If you need anything, he'll be around to help."

Eddie looked thrilled to have found someplace for Derek to go, but Derek didn't care. He just wanted somewhere he could sleep, veg out and hopefully write a song or two.

"How does your friend's foreman feel about babysitting me?" He rolled over on to his back, studying the tiles on the ceiling.

"Les said he was fine with it." Eddie put his hand on Derek's arm. "So you'll go?"

"Sure. Why not?"

Derek laughed. Hell, he was a country singer who'd never spent time out in the country or on a ranch. It might be interesting to see an actual working ranch. All those cowboys would be food for fantasy and song.

Chapter Two

RM Ranch, Wyoming

Max Furlo watched Les Hardin's truck pull into the drive with more resignation than surprise. Brody had told him some guy was going to come and stay for a while. Brody and Tony were heading for Germany, so they were letting the guy crash at their place. He didn't care as long as the man wasn't expecting Max to entertain him.

The truck stopped and Les stepped out, looking around. Max grimaced, but moved on the porch of the foreman's house. He saw the smile and nod Les sent him.

It never ceased to amaze him how the foursome of Les and Randy, Brody and Tony, had opened their homes and lives to him without asking for anything in return. He thought for a moment—they had asked something of him. They wanted him to never destroy their trust. Brody and Tony probably wondered what an Aussie cowboy was doing so far from home, but they'd never pestered him with questions.

"Max," Les called as the passenger climbed out of the truck.

Max froze and thought God must really hate him. With an angel's voice and a body built to fulfil every fantasy Max might have, Derek St Martin stood in the driveway. Max knew he was being punished for some sin he'd committed in a former life.

"Les." Max strolled towards Les, shaking the man's hand. "The big house is clean. Margie and Randy left for your place about ten minutes ago."

Derek pulled a battered guitar case and a suitcase from the back of Les' truck.

"Great. Derek, this is Max Furlo. He's the foreman around here." Les introduced them.

"Foreman? Is that like a manager?" Derek smiled, but the lighthearted expression didn't show in his eyes.

"Yes."

Max wasn't about to start babbling like a schoolgirl, just because the most gorgeous man he'd ever seen was standing in front of him. Derek's face registered surprise at Max's short answer. Les laughed.

"Edward said you wanted peace and quiet, Derek. You'll get it here. Max isn't much of a talker and he'll be busy with the bulls." Les slapped Max on the shoulder. "Can you show Derek around? I've got to get home and help Randy finish packing."

"Sure."

Max and Derek watched as Les jumped back in the truck and drove off. The silence grew until Max sighed. He gestured to the suitcase and guitar.

"Do you need help?"

Derek shook his head. "No, I've got them. Thanks for letting me stay."

"It's not my ranch. The bosses say you stay, you stay." Max led the way to the big house.

"Still, it can't be fun for you to have me here." Derek followed him in.

"Do you need entertaining?" He grabbed the set of keys Tony had left on the stand next to the door.

"No." The singer studied him.

"Then we'll get along fine." He tossed Derek the keys. "House and truck. Refrigerator's full, along with the pantry. Room's at the top of the stairs. First one on your left. Enjoy."

Max tipped his hat, turned around and left.

He walked slowly away. He didn't want Derek to think he was running from him. Max got inside his own house then went upstairs to take a cold shower.

Shit, he was going to have to stay far away from Derek St Martin. The country singer was straight as an arrow and Max didn't want to make either of them uncomfortable by sporting a hard-on every time they were around each other.

The cold water wasn't helping, so he switched it over to hot, soaped his hand and imagined his fist was a pretty mouth wrapped around his cock. Max pumped slowly at first, seeing bright blue eyes staring up at him as he looked down. He growled and tightened his grip on his dick.

Shit! He sped up, stroking faster as his climax built. It had been a few days since he'd taken the time to jerk off. After seeing the bosses' houseguest, Max had a feeling he'd be doing it a lot more often.

He changed the image in his mind to Derek leaning over and Max fucking his ass hard and fast. In his daydream it didn't matter that Derek St Martin was as straight as a ruler. In his dream, the man was calling his name, begging him to fuck him.

"Fuck!" Max shouted as he came, spilling cum over his hand and onto the tiles of the shower. He braced his other hand on the wall to keep from collapsing while he milked every drop from his cock.

When he could breathe normally again, Max rinsed before shutting off the shower. He dried off using the towel he'd hung on the rack, and laughed at his reflection in the mirror. Hell, if there were any clues St Martin would even be interested in him, Max would offer up a summer fling in a heartbeat.

He padded into his bedroom, and stood for a moment, stretching. His spine cracked and creaked as he bent to grab a pair of sweats from the floor. It was time for dinner in front of the TV. Maybe there'd be a baseball game on.

* * * *

Derek frowned as the foreman left. The man was in a huge hurry to be gone.

Les Hardin had promised he wouldn't be bothered and it was obvious that while Max might not care if Derek was there or not, he certainly wasn't going to go out of his way to be friendly.

He went upstairs, following Max's directions. His room was done in blues and whites, with white pine furniture. A few pictures hung on the walls featuring horses and cowboys. He set his suitcase on the bed and propped his guitar against the footboard. He thought he'd get something to eat before crashing.

He'd never explained to Eddie that the worst part of his last eight-month tour was the crush he'd developed on his new bass player. He'd had to guard against any inappropriate behaviour on his part. He'd go to his hotel room and take some pills or drink to knock himself out. For the first time since they'd started touring together, he didn't go out with the band, but it hadn't stopped his growing dependence on manmade substances to get him through the shows.

Shaking his head, he tried to stop thinking about it. No need to be watchful here. First, no one knew he was at the ranch and second, Eddie had said Les, Randy, Brody and Tony were gay, plus they were pretty open about it to the hands who worked for them. If anyone realised he liked guys, they wouldn't hassle him.

It was time to stop whining and get a grip on his life. No one was forcing Derek to take the drugs and drink. He was the only one pouring the liquor and popping the pills. He was an adult, responsible for his own actions, which meant admitting he was the only one to blame for where he found himself now.

The RM Ranch would be his first step to control. He would make a plan and organise his life. He had other issues to deal with besides his health and addictions. Other things weren't adding up and he needed time to decide what to do about those as well.

Derek glanced out of his window and noticed Max standing in an upstairs room of the smaller house across the lawn. Shit. The man was naked. Darkness had fallen and Max's body was silhouetted in the window.

"Look away, Derek. Bad way to start your stay." He averted his eyes and moved out of the bedroom.

Denying himself had become second nature to him. He went downstairs to the kitchen, feeling like he'd crashed someone's life. Photos covered the walls. They seemed to be following the lives of two young men. Both were handsome and smiling. One was blond, the other Hispanic. Derek wondered who they were. He fixed a sandwich and wandered through the rooms, checking out the framed pictures.

A large photo hung over the stone fireplace and he stopped to study it. He recognised Brody MacCafferty. The other, older man looked familiar. Moving closer, he studied his face, but he couldn't place the guy. He'd done some promos for the PBR and he knew Tony Romanos was a bull rider. Maybe that was where he thought he knew him from. Brody and Tony stood with their arms around each other, love obvious in their smiles. Two younger men sat in front of them.

Derek wondered if anyone knew those two kids were in love as well. He could tell by the way the darker kid leaned into the blond, like he needed to touch him.

"What an interesting family," he murmured.

After cleaning up his dishes, he stepped outside. It'd been a long time since he'd been anywhere he could look up and actually see stars. There was a wooden swing hanging at one end of the porch. He ran back inside and grabbed a blanket. He curled up on the swing and soaked in the silence.

It didn't matter if he didn't go to sleep right away. There wasn't anything he needed to do tomorrow. Maybe the best thing for him was simply letting his body get so tired, it went to sleep on its own, instead of using pills or alcohol.

A twinge of hope rose in him. Maybe Eddie was right. This might be the perfect place for him to rest and write songs. Music drifted over his ears on the night breeze. It wasn't loud or obnoxious. In fact, it sounded like someone was playing a guitar for real.

Derek thought about investigating, but his body was happy where it was. He drifted asleep to the gentle music.

* * * *

"Three a.m.," Max muttered, looking at the alarm clock that sat on the stand next to his bed.

Max crawled out from under the covers. He wondered if he'd ever sleep an entire night. Tugging on a pair of jeans, he made his way down to his kitchen.

His body had got used to existing on a few hours of sleep. It had been that way since he was a kid. Max's kitchen window faced the back of the big house. He frowned when he saw a bundle on the porch swing.

Grumbling a little, he pulled on his boots and headed over to see what it was. As he reached out to touch it, the blanket moved and Derek's auburn curls were revealed.

Max's hand hung in the air. He didn't want to wake the guy up because he really didn't want to talk to him. He remembered the impression he'd got of Derek being all lean muscle. Sleeping out on the swing would be hell on the man's back and the summer air held a bit of a chill.

"St Martin."

Derek mumbled and shifted, the blanket falling to uncover the man's chest. A tight white T-shirt hid Derek's Adonis body from Max's gaze.

"Hey, Derek, wake up." He tried again, not wanting to touch him.

Derek's blue eyes blinked open. Once. Twice. A small smile graced the man's tired face. "It's so quiet here. I must have fallen asleep."

He pushed the blanket to his waist and stretched. Max averted his eyes — he was afraid he'd start whimpering. The white fabric rode up a little, giving him a peek of a trail of hair leading down under Derek's sweatpants.

"You'll get stiff." His cheeks heated and he said a silent word of thanks for the shadows he stood in.

"Yeah. It's been a long time since I've slept on anything harder than a mattress." Derek uncurled, standing up.

Max's mouth went dry and he couldn't say anything to that comment. He found himself staring directly into Derek's eyes. They were the same height, which would make kissing Derek damn near perfect, and their bodies would line up nicely, if they were to get up close and personal that way.

Derek moved to the left and strolled to the door. Max watched the sway of the man's ass, thinking Derek could teach a class on how to entice with just his hips.

"Would you like a cup of coffee? Now that I'm up, I won't get back to sleep for a while. Unless I break out the pills or whisky." Derek flashed him a smile. "And I'm trying not to do that anymore."

Max's heart skipped. *Don't read anything into it*, he told himself sternly. There had never been even a whisper of doubt as to Derek's sexuality. *You're setting yourself up for heartache.*

"Okay." His agreement shocked him and surprised Derek, if the wide-eyed look he received was any indication.

"Good. I did figure out the coffeemaker. One thing I can't live without."

Max followed Derek to the kitchen.

"What's the story with these guys?" Derek gestured to the family photo over the mantel.

He didn't gossip. Never found the use for it. "The bosses and a younger brother and a nephew."

Derek looked at him. "Les said you wouldn't talk my ear off. Good to see he was right."

Max sat at the table while he watched the man putter around and make the coffee.

"Not much of a talker, huh?" Derek pushed the plate of cookies Les' housekeeper, Margie, had baked as a welcome present towards him.

"Nothing important enough to say worth wasting air for."

He took one. He didn't eat sweets usually, but he needed to keep his hands busy.

Derek's laugh was low and hit him right in the groin. He moaned.

"These are great. Who baked them?"

Max thanked his lucky stars Derek thought he was moaning over the cookies. "Les' housekeeper. You'll meet her eventually."

"Really?" Derek got up and poured two cups of coffee.

"She'll be over here, making sure you don't need anything."

Max took a swig. Black and strong, just how he liked it.

"Australian," Derek crowed.

He glanced up.

"I've been trying to place your accent, but you didn't use long enough sentences for me to figure it out. What are you doing here?" Derek tucked his feet under him and rested his elbows on his knees.

Max had never seen such a flexible man. He forced his mind away from all the erotic images that thought caused to flash through his mind.

"I needed a change of scenery." He traced the rim of his mug.

"Not running from a broken heart?"

Again he squashed the burst of hope in his heart. Derek wasn't fishing.

"No. It was time to move on."

"Is everyone on these two ranches gay?"

Derek's question was soft and Max wasn't sure if he'd heard him right.

"What?"

Derek's eyes were serious and held an emotion Max couldn't name.

"I wanted to know if everyone who worked here was gay."

"A few. Most are straight but don't care what goes on between adults." He was proud of his casual answer.

"What about the younger brother and nephew? They in love?"

"No business of yours."

Derek grinned. "You're right. It's not. I'm just curious. Eddie would say my curiosity is going to get me in trouble someday."

"Eddie?" Max wanted to bite his tongue. This was the second-longest conversation he'd had in a year.

"Edward Monterrose. He's my best friend and my stepbrother. He was the one who suggested I come here." Derek jumped to his feet, moving around the kitchen in a spurt of energy. "I needed a place to crash. I've been on tour for eight months. I'm running on empty."

Max grunted. "Doesn't look like it."

Derek chuckled and heat stiffened Max's cock.

"I know. Outside on the swing was the most sleep I've gotten in several days without help of drugs." Derek rested a slender hip against the counter and stared out of the window. "I can see doing a lot of sleeping around here."

"Not much to do...unless you ride?" He posed the last part as a question.

"Eddie's a rider. I needed to learn just to keep up with him. I'm not an expert, but I can stay on."

He nodded. Maybe he'd offer to take the guy riding after the newness and exhaustion wore off. An easy silence settled over them. He wouldn't have broken the quiet, even if it had got awkward. He could go days without speaking unless absolutely necessary.

The singer picked up the pot and held it out to Max, asking without words if he wanted more. He shook his head. Any more and he would be up the rest of the night. Unlike Derek, he needed to be up early to check on the horses and cattle. Derek filled his own cup, humming. Max wondered if Derek even realised what he was doing.

Derek patted his shirt like he was looking for something he expected to be there. A rueful smile crossed the singer's face.

"Want a smoke?" Max had seen Tony make the same gesture when his boss was looking for a cigarette.

"Yeah, but I quit two months ago. Just haven't gotten out of the habit." Derek winked. "My manager said they were bad for my voice."

Max knew it was none of his business, but he couldn't help saying, "Yet the alcohol and drugs are acceptable?"

A grimace twisted Derek's thin lips. "Fucked up, isn't it?"

"Yeah." Max checked the clock on the stove. "I have to be up in three hours. I need to grab some more sleep."

"Thanks for waking me up, man." Derek grabbed Max's cup and rinsed it out before setting it in the sink.

"No problem. You'd be stiff in the morning if I didn't." Standing, Max turned to head for the front door. He stopped before leaving the kitchen. "There's a pack of cigarettes in the cupboard over the microwave. Smoking might be the least of all the evils."

He left, not allowing Derek to stop him or say anything. It was going to be hard enough falling back asleep after seeing the singer in sweats that showed off a lot of the man's ass.

"Not for you, boy-o," he muttered as he let himself back into his house. Straight or not, Derek St Martin wouldn't be interested in a regular old cowboy with nothing special to offer anyone.

Chapter Three

The blaring of a horn shot Derek out of bed. He landed on the floor in a tangle of blankets and sheets, shooting looks around him. After three days of mostly sleeping and very little eating, he still hadn't got used to waking up in this room.

"What the fuck?"

Rolling around, he managed to free his feet and stood up, heading towards the window. Right before he reached it, he remembered he was naked. He tugged on the sweats he'd thrown over the chair. He pushed the curtains out of the way to see Max stride across the yard, brown cowboy hat tugged low and anger apparent in each step.

He cracked the window enough to hear Max yell at the kid standing outside the blue truck. The kid had his arm through the driver's window and pressed on the horn.

"God damn, Jasper, I told you not to come around here anymore." Max grabbed the kid's arm and pulled him away from the truck. "There are people still trying to sleep."

Jasper swayed. "Where is he, Max? I just want to talk to him."

Derek didn't need to be anywhere near the kid to know Jasper was drunk.

"Shit, Jasper. When did you start drinking?" Max covered his nose with his hand.

"Last night. I need to see him." The kid grasped Max's shirt and stared earnestly up at him.

"Yancey's not here. You have to stop stalking him. You're going to get your ass in trouble." Max stepped back, dislodging Jasper's hand.

Jasper stumbled and would have kissed the ground with his face if Max hadn't caught him. Derek shook his head. It had been a long time since he'd got that drunk. He'd learnt just how much he needed to drink to fall asleep and had always tried to stick to that amount. Of course, he hadn't been in love for a long time either. Love made a person do stupid things.

"Where did he go, Max?"

"It doesn't matter, kid." Max gestured to someone out of Derek's sight. "Tip, get your ass over here."

A stocky, grey-haired man strolled up. "Yeah, boss?"

"Drive Jasper home. Make sure he gets there okay. Have Abe follow you so you have a ride home." Max handed Jasper off to the shorter man.

"Okay." Tip started to ease the kid towards the truck.

"Where is Yancey, Max? Don't lie to me." Jasper jerked away from Tip and swung.

Derek held his breath. How would the big foreman react to the kid's attack? Max ducked the punch and grabbed Jasper's shoulder, whirling the kid around to push him at Tip.

"He's in Europe, Jasper. Meeting Juan and hanging out with him." Max shook his head. "You've got to get over this. Yancey's in love with Juan and has been for years. I know he told you that."

Jasper's face crumpled and Derek wondered if the kid was crying. Tip led Jasper to his truck and helped him into the passenger side. The men drove off with another red truck following them. Max stood in the yard, jerked his hat off his head and shoved his hand through his hair.

The thought of that hand stroking over his skin stiffened Derek's cock. Max's gaze shot up and met Derek's through the window, like the foreman knew what Derek was thinking. He hoped the distance was great enough for Max not to notice the lust on Derek's face.

He dropped the curtain and turned, heading towards the bathroom. He dug out jeans, a jock and a T-shirt on his way. No one cared how he dressed here. Jeans and T-shirt looked like the uniform of choice. His boots were still downstairs.

They hadn't much to do with each other since that late night chat when Derek had first arrived at the ranch. Max respected Derek's need to rest and had only stopped in once the day before to make sure he was still okay. Not having anyone make demands on his time was a novelty to Derek, letting him enjoy the silence for a while. Now that he was up, he found himself wanting to know more about the ranch and its handsome foreman.

A knock sounded on the bathroom door as he finished brushing his teeth.

"Yeah?" He opened the door.

Max stood in the hallway. Derek felt an odd rush of pride at the way Max's eyes widened and the quick but thorough head-to-toe glance Max gave him.

"Breakfast is ready, if you want some." Max jerked a thumb over his shoulder towards the stairs.

Derek frowned. God, how long had it been since he'd actually eaten breakfast? It had to have been since he started touring. On tour, he rarely got to bed before three and would wake up at two the next afternoon in time for sound check at the next venue. Also, a month into the tour, his stomach was so screwed up, he could barely eat plain toast and milk.

"You made breakfast?"

He followed Max downstairs, trying like hell not to stare at the tight bubble butt in front of him. Max's jeans were faded at the seams and he wore them comfortably. Derek wondered what he looked like naked. Tight muscles flexing and moving as he thrust into Max's ass. He stumbled slightly and caught himself. Shit. Thomas would be pissed if he injured himself because he imagined another guy naked.

Derek concentrated so hard on not staring at Max, he didn't notice him stop until Derek squashed his face into Max's back.

"Umph," he grunted. "Damn."

"Are you okay?" Max turned and gripped Derek's arms to steady him.

"Yeah. Sorry. I wasn't paying attention." Derek's cheeks heated and he knew he was blushing.

"No problem. Probably still groggy. Sorry Jasper woke you up."

Derek wanted to protest when Max let go of Derek's arms and stepped back. He missed the warm rough hands on his skin.

"I should be up anyway. Shouldn't waste another day sleeping." He grinned. "Something smells good. Did you really cook breakfast?"

"I've been up for four hours. Had coffee and toast when I got up, but I usually come up here at ten for breakfast with the bosses. They tell me what they want done the rest of the day. Brody cooks because Tony can't cook worth shit. At least nothing more exciting than pancakes."

It seemed like Max was almost babbling. Derek wondered if he'd caught the foreman on a bad day that first day, or if Max was more relaxed in the morning. Did Max wake up slow or fast? Derek doubted he'd ever learn the answer to that question.

"Mac's a pretty good cook. He made a few meals for me when he was guarding me." Derek leaned against the doorframe, watching Max move around the kitchen.

"Coffee?" Max held up the pot.

"Sure. Do you have orange juice?" Derek wanted to start cutting back on his caffeine intake. It would help settle his stomach and he hoped he would sleep better at night.

"Don't know. Randy and Margie stocked the kitchen for you. There might be some in the fridge."

Derek went to look while Max pulled out a cup and poured the coffee. There was orange juice and milk, plus a huge variety of food. He'd have to think about cooking again. He pulled the juice out and shut the door. Sneaking a peek in the freezer, he saw some steaks. He grabbed them and set them on the counter.

"Want to join me for dinner tonight? I'll cook."

Max nodded. "Sure."

"What time can you usually call it good for the night?" He sat at the table in the small nook of the kitchen and smiled when Max set a full plate in front of him.

"Evening feed is around seven. I can be here at seven-thirty." Max sat down.

"Cool." Derek tried not to think he'd just made a date with a sexy cowboy.

They spent the next few minutes eating. Derek's stomach didn't twinge once at the food. Maybe because for the first time, it was filled with something other than narcotics.

After taking the edge off his hunger, he picked up his orange juice and took a drink. "Tell me Jasper's story."

Max frowned.

"I know you don't like to talk or gossip about your employers. I respect that, but I don't plan on saying anything to anyone." Derek gestured to himself. "I'm the least likely to talk."

"He's obsessed with Brody's younger brother, Yancey. Yancey never encouraged the kid. Hell, Yancey's been in love with Juan, Tony's nephew, since they met." Max stared into his cup.

"Yancey's told him this?"

"Sure. Jasper followed him everywhere. Never gave him a moment's peace. Finally, Yancey told him about Juan." Max snorted. "Didn't do a bit of good. Jasper figured Yancey was lonely because of Juan living out East for the last couple of years."

"It must be hard on Yancey. Being alone with the guy you love so far away." Derek heard the hint of a melody dancing in his head.

"Alone is easy. Lonely is hard. There's a difference."

The words hit Derek hard. Music echoed in his mind and words to the song shot through his brain. He leapt to his feet and Max stared at him.

"I have to write that down."

Derek raced to his room, grabbing his guitar and his lyric book. A song poured from his soul. A soul he thought had withered and dried up under the stage lights of his career.

* * * *

Max watched Derek run from the kitchen. He wondered what had struck the singer, but Max understood artists. His mother had been one and he'd dated a few. There was no fighting inspiration when it hit.

He cleared the table, rinsing the dishes before he stuck them in the dishwasher. The steaks went on a plate in the refrigerator. He wasn't sure if Derek's creativity would play itself out by dinnertime. Max planned on showing up just in case.

After grabbing his hat from the hook by the door, he stepped outside. He tugged it down to shade his eyes. Bright blue skies framed the Rockies. So different from his native Australia, but a lot of things were the same. Wild and untamed, the mountains throwing their huge shadow over the land.

The small similarities to his homeland were one of the reasons why he'd come to Wyoming. The other reason was he'd heard about Les Hardin, and his tendency to take in strays. Max had been looking for a place to work for a couple of weeks, so when Brody and Tony had offered him the foreman job on their ranch, he couldn't pass it up.

He'd been working on the ranch for a couple of years, but he never got tired of the view. Max wanted to yell to Derek, to bring the singer outside and share the view. He shook his head. *Let him write.* Max said he wouldn't crowd the man and Derek didn't need to be entertained.

Max headed down to the barns. He had some yearlings to work with.

Chapter Four

Derek stared at the notebook in front of him. He blinked back the tears threatening to fall. *Don't be a silly fool.*

So many nights spent staring at blank pages and holding his guitar. So many days waiting for words to match notes and his songs to come again.

His first song in two years. Two simple sentences from a gorgeous cowboy had spawned what he thought could be one of his best songs ever. Derek decided to dedicate it to Jasper, because he understood what the kid was going through.

Putting his guitar away, he glanced at the clock next to the bed. Five o'clock. He'd been working since eleven. His stomach growled, reminding him he missed lunch. Standing, he stretched and listened to the vertebrae popping in his back. God, he loved the feeling of accomplishing or creating beauty through the words of a song.

Derek went downstairs to the kitchen. He grabbed an apple from the fridge, spotting the steaks. Shit. He'd forgotten about dinner with Max. He'd better apologise for running out on him and make sure the cowboy still wanted to eat together.

He tugged on his boots and headed outside. The smell of horses, dust and hay hit his nose. Filling his lungs with the intriguing scents, Derek remembered them from the times he'd gone to the stables with Eddie.

An older grey-haired cowboy walked towards Derek.

"Excuse me, can you tell me where I can find Max?"

The man eyed him for a moment before he nodded. "Boss is in the yearling barn."

Derek's confusion must have shown on his face because the ranch hand turned and pointed to the line of barns.

"Yearlings are in the last barn. You the big bosses' friend staying up at the main house?"

"Yes." Derek wondered how much the ranch hands knew about him.

"Furlo said you were a good one, just looking for a place to stay for a while." The man smiled.

"Thanks."

Strolling towards the last barn, he glanced back over his shoulder and saw the cowboy walking away. Did the men here really not know who he was? Had they kept his identity from everyone or were these people willing to respect his privacy?

Stopping in the doorway, he bit back the greeting he was about to call out. Max stood in the wide aisle with his arms wrapped around a shorter, blond man. Derek shifted, not wanting to interrupt the couple.

Max's head came up and his dark brown eyes met Derek's. Derek could tell the anger in them wasn't directed at him.

"I'll come back later," he mouthed to Max.

Max shook his head and gestured for Derek to come closer. As Derek edged nearer, Max leant down and whispered something to the blond.

The smaller man stepped away, wiping his cheeks as he turned around to face Derek. Derek thought it interesting Max kept his arm around the blond's waist, yet the look on Max's face spoke more of protective emotions than lust.

A shy smile graced the younger man's face, chasing away the sadness. A thin elegant hand reached out to Derek.

"I'm Peter Skinner."

Derek shook Peter's hand and grinned. "I'm Derek St Martin."

"I know. Les told me you were staying here. I was going to stop by in a few days to see how you were doing and if you needed anything." Peter tucked his hands in his pockets. "I'm Les' accountant," he explained.

"I'm good so far. Max has been taking care of me." He winked at Max.

Damn, if the man didn't blush, and that was interesting. Derek hadn't pegged Max as a guy who'd be interested in men. Of course, he never had that magic sense called 'gaydar', so he was sure he missed signals from most guys.

"I was just double-checking with Max about dinner. Would you like to join us? I can thaw another steak quick."

Peter shook his head and smiled shyly. "Thanks, but I have to get back to the ranch. Les likes to have the bills paid on time."

"I know how that is." A thought struck him. "You're probably busy, but I was wondering if you'd look over my accounts for me."

"You think there might be a problem?" Peter's interest was definitely piqued, and it made Derek feel good to push away the man's palpable sadness, if only for a few moments.

"I've had my suspicions for a while. I've got all the files and everything, but numbers aren't my things. Do you think you'll have time to look them over? I can have them overnighted, if it works for you." Derek figured it was a way to solve a problem for both of them...something about his financials had been bugging him for at least three months, at least when he was sober enough to worry about it.

"Max can get you the address." Peter checked his watch. "Les said he'd call me in an hour and I should have answers to some of his questions."

Derek nodded and grinned when Peter pushed up on tiptoes, brushing a kiss over Max's cheek. "Thanks, Max."

The red in Max's face deepened. "Anytime, kid."

They watched Peter leave the barn.

"Cute kid," Derek commented.

Max shot Derek a quick glance. "Didn't think you went that way."

Derek snorted. "Shit, even if I didn't, I hope I have enough confidence to admit another guy's good-looking." He ducked his head and his shoulders tensed. "Thomas told me when I signed my first record deal, I couldn't be gay. So I'm not—in public, at least."

Max's boots came into view before a hand landed on his shoulder. Meeting Max's sympathetic gaze, Derek felt his muscles relax.

"I get why he said that, but I don't think I'd like your manager if I met him."

He appreciated Max's quiet support. "Yeah. The older I get, the less I like him myself."

Since he wasn't on the ranch to hit on cowboys, he tried not to think about how good Max's hand felt on his body.

"I came out to tell you I'm sorry for running off like that at breakfast. Something you said triggered a song idea for me."

"I've known a few artists and understand about taking advantage of inspiration when it strikes."

Derek leaned against one of the stalls as Max led a gangly black horse from it. "It's been two years since I've written anything."

"Had to be hard."

Max clipped the cross-ties to the black's halter. Derek watched him run his hands over the filly's back, down her long legs and lift each hoof.

"It was like having a part of my soul amputated," he admitted. "What are you doing?"

"Getting her used to human touch. She's friendly, but still a little flighty. She'll outgrow that." He picked a brush out of a box and, with long firm strokes, made the filly's coat shine.

"Is she going to be sold?" Derek kept his eyes on the filly, willing his cock not to swell.

The flex and roll of Max's muscles under his dark green T-shirt teased Derek. Dark patches of sweat and dirt streaked Max's clothes as well. How much dirtier could he get Max if he jumped him right there? He fought back a moan. Fuck, maybe coming out here wasn't a good idea.

"We have six yearlings in the barn. Five are heading for a sale in the fall."

Derek closed his eyes, shutting out the sight of Max's tight ass covered by worn jeans as Max bent over to clean one of the filly's hooves.

"What are you going to do with the one you're not selling?"

Max murmured to the filly while he moved to her other side. Dark eyes met Derek's and an emotion flashed in them he couldn't decipher.

"When she's old enough, she'll head over to Hersch for training as a cutting horse."

Checking his watch, Derek wondered what a cutting horse was. "I better go in and get dinner started."

"I'll clean up and be there in a few."

Derek made it to the large sliding barn door before breaking down and looking back. Max stood, arm thrown across the filly's back. His gaze hit Derek's groin, letting Derek know Max had been staring at his ass. Max took his time raising his eyes. Derek was throbbing by the time Max looked him in the eye. A quirk of a dark eyebrow and a nod told Derek Max liked what he saw. Derek winked and left.

* * * *

Max stood outside the back door of the big house. He knocked on it before opening it and stepping in. Derek peeked around the corner.

"Right on time. The steaks just got off the grill and the potatoes are done."

"Smells good." Max toed off his boots and hung his hat on the rack next to the door.

"I sautéed some mushrooms to put on the steaks. You want to get the drinks?"

Derek held two plates full of food and nodded to the glasses on the counter. Max grabbed a beer for himself and a soda for Derek from the fridge, opened the bottles and followed Derek into the dining room.

There were two place settings at one end of the oak table. He set the drinks down and pulled out a chair for Derek. Max grinned when Derek's face registered surprise.

Derek chuckled. "Are you going to be nice to me now?"

"I'm sorry about that first night. I was tired and not very happy about having to babysit anyone. It didn't matter who it was." Max shrugged. "I like your music and think you're bloody gorgeous, but I have a ranch to run, plus helping Jackson out at Hardin's place if he needs me."

"Jackson?"

Derek took a drink and didn't comment on the fact Max had got him soda instead of a beer. Max tried not to think about how that pretty mouth would look wrapped around his cock. Shit, now he had a boner. Shifting, he searched for more room in his jeans.

"Jackson is Hardin's foreman and Hersch's future brother-in-law, whenever Hersch's bastard of a father dies."

"Hersch…that's Randy, right?"

Max nodded.

"Just trying to get everyone straight. So his dad is a bit of asshole, huh?"

"The world will be a better place when the man dies." He scowled at his plate.

"Does he harass Randy and Les because they're gay?"

"It's only one of many reasons Robert has for hating Randy. The man hates all his children and most every other person in the world."

Max sighed. He couldn't believe how mean and nasty Robert Hersch was. Silence settled in for several minutes while they ate. When most of the food was gone, Derek glanced up.

"Eddie told me Les and Randy met when Randy had a fight with Robert. Les took him in, right?"

"Yeah. If you go over to their ranch, you'll notice the extra people hanging around. Hardin picks up strays like dogs get fleas. He has a big house and a big heart, which is good, because Peter is going to need a place to stay."

"Was that why he was here?" Derek's tone was casual. "Are you seeing each other?"

Max choked. "Hell no. Peter's a good kid, though it's strange to call him a kid. He's twenty-six, the same age as Hersch, but Peter hasn't seen any of the world except what's around here."

He pushed his empty plate away and rested his elbows on the table, running his fingers around the lip of his bottle.

"I'm the only one around right now and he needed someone to talk to about his grandfather. I wonder if it's in the water."

"Another ass?"

Derek stood, picking their plates up and carrying them to the kitchen. Max followed.

"He's pissed because Peter's working for Hardin. After being around those guys, he got the courage to 'come out' to his family and they kicked him out."

"Is everyone around here either gay or fucked up?" Derek rinsed the plates before stuffing them in the dishwasher.

"It sounds like it, but for the most part, people are pretty decent. Live and let live as long as you're not hurting anyone. As for the gay part, you happen to be staying on a ranch owned by two gay men whose best friends are gay and live down the road. It's going to seem like there are a lot more gay men here than normal."

He rested a hip against the counter and watched Derek move. Did dance lessons cause the singer to move so gracefully or if was natural?

"His grandfather told Peter he could come back if he stopped being gay. Like it's a damn switch he can turn on and off. Peter came over to ask me what he should do."

After drying his hands, Derek tossed the towel back on the counter. Max fought a smile as Derek pulled out a pack of cigarettes from the cupboard.

"See you found the smokes," he teased, nodding towards the pack.

"I figured you were right. Smoking calms me better than drinking or drugs do. I'd rather risk getting lung cancer than overdosing." Derek gestured to the back porch. "Care to join me?"

Max placed their empty bottles in a box by the door and grabbed two sodas from the fridge. "I don't smoke. Never picked up the habit, I guess."

He handed a soda to Derek and sat on the second step. Derek leaned against the railing. Twilight settled in with a last faint streak of orange painting the black velvet sky as the sun set behind the mountains. The horses and cattle had been fed and bedded down.

Max decided long ago that sunset was his favourite time of day. It meant he could finally relax a little. With full darkness, he couldn't do anything except wait for morning to arrive.

"It's beautiful," Derek murmured, his deep intake of smoke and air breaking the quiet.

"Yes." Max braced himself on his elbows, coming inches from Derek's bare feet. "Don't wander barefoot too much. Stones, bugs and snakes can get you."

"Thanks for the warning." Derek nudged him with a foot. "What'd you tell him?"

"What could I tell him? I said each of us has our own road to take to where we're happy with ourselves. He has to decide if being separated from his family is worth being out or if being happy means hiding who he is. Sappy, huh?"

His cheeks warm, Max was glad the darkness hid the blush from Derek. He moved restlessly. God, he didn't remember ever feeling this awkward with anyone, not even when he'd met his estranged father's family for the first time.

"Sappy? Nah, it's the truth."

They sank into silence again. Max enjoyed the simple rhythm of Derek's breathing. A few minutes later, Derek started humming. The man had natural talent. His voice wasn't created in some mixing studio, Max thought. Derek stopped.

"Something new?" He tilted his head back to look up at Derek. Eyes closed, Derek nodded.

"I'm getting words along with bits and pieces of melody. It'll come together eventually. More than likely at two in the morning and drag me out of a sound sleep."

Derek didn't sound too upset by that thought.

"My mum used to say her muse never slept. It spent all its time thinking of ways to drive her crazy."

Joy and sadness mingled in his heart at the memories he had of waking up to find his mother, splattered with paint, curled up, asleep, on the floor of her studio.

"What did your mom do?" Derek sat next to Max, mirroring his posture.

"She painted and sketched. She used every kind of medium she could. God, she loved art. Even at her worst, right before she died, she was drawing." He smiled.

"How long ago did you lose her?" Derek seemed hesitant to ask.

"Nine years ago. She died of cancer."

And maybe finally of a broken heart.

"Sorry to hear that. You must have loved her a lot." Derek brushed his shoulder against Max.

"I did." He didn't want to talk about his family anymore. "What about your parents? Are they still around?"

"They're both still alive, if that's what you mean. Out jet-setting around the world, I'm sure. We're not close, as you can tell. Only Eddie and I stay in touch and it's for the best."

Max could tell Derek was reluctant to talk about his family as well. He realised he didn't want the night to end.

"Hey, would you like to come over and watch a movie?" He gestured towards his house.

Derek's wide smile made Max grin in return.

"Sure, let me put on some shoes."

Max pulled on his own boots and hat, standing outside to wait for Derek. *You're heading for trouble.* Hell, he risked getting his heart broken.

There was something about Derek St Martin that spoke to Max on a deeper level than just attraction. He could fall in love with the country singer.

It was going to hurt when Derek's vacation ended and he left. Max had no illusions about that, but he also realised he didn't want to miss the opportunity to love Derek. He'd seen the hints of interest and lust in Derek's gaze. If it was only a summer fling, Max was going to ride it for as long as Derek was here.

Chapter Five

Ringing woke Max up the next day. He rolled over to check the clock. Ten minutes before his alarm was set to go off. He was tempted to ignore the phone, but it was probably one of his bosses checking in.

"Hello," he grunted, sitting up.

"Hey Furlo, how's it going?"

Damn, Romanos sounded chipper.

"What time is it where you are?"

Romanos laughed. "Not sure. Must be close to five at night. Why?"

"Just wondering." Max scrubbed a hand over his face.

"How's things going? St Martin settle in okay?"

There was noise in the background. Max could make out MacCafferty's voice.

"He's good. Hasn't annoyed me yet."

He thought about how he'd enjoyed watching *Hitman* with Derek last night. Definitely not annoying.

"Great."

"Tell Yancey Jasper hasn't given up. The kid stopped by yesterday, drunk and looking for him."

He didn't want to tell Romanos, but figured Yancey had the right to know.

"Thanks. Stupid kid can't take a hint." Romanos sighed.

"Hardin needs to call Peter." Max pushed his blankets off and stood. Stretching, he thought about the conversation he had yesterday with Peter.

"Les is talking to Peter right now. Thanks for watching out for him." Sadness tainted Romanos' voice.

"He's a good kid." Max wandered over to the window. "Customer called yesterday as well. He's interested in buying a yearling, but he's willing to wait and talk to you when you get back."

Glancing outside, he grunted in surprise.

"What?"

He'd forgotten Romanos was still on the line.

"Your guest is up already."

Derek sat on the big house's front steps, guitar in his arms and a notebook beside him.

"Really? After talking to Monterrose, I'd have thought the man would spend all his time sleeping."

Max smiled when Derek lit a cigarette. "Must be all this fresh air."

"Yeah. Gotta go. I'll give you a call sometime next week."

Tossing the phone on the bed as he went by, Max headed for the shower.

Fifteen minutes later, he walked out of his house with two mugs of coffee. Derek glanced up when the screen door slammed and smiled at Max around the pencil clutched in his teeth.

"Coffee?"

He sat a mug down next to Derek and crouched. Derek nodded, but didn't stop playing. There was something off about the chord Derek struck on the strings.

Without thinking, Max said, "Maybe you should put an F there instead of a G."

Derek frowned. After a moment's hesitation, he changed the note and the melody sounded better. He stopped, pulled the pencil from his mouth and scribbled something down. He eyed Max with a speculative stare.

"You play the guitar?"

Max gave a 'so-so' gesture. "Well enough for people to know what I'm playing."

"What about singing?" Derek pursed his lips.

"I can sing, but not as well as you. At least dogs don't howl when I open my mouth."

He nodded at Derek to keep playing.

Derek sang softly. *Must be a new song,* Max thought, sipping his coffee and appreciating Derek's clear baritone voice.

As Derek finished, the first ranch hands started arriving. Half of the guys lived in town or had their own places. They made extra income by working on the RM.

Max eased to his feet, his knees protesting. "I have to help with the feeding and assign guys their work for the day. After that, I plan on checking fence line. Would you like to ride with me?"

He took the empty mug Derek handed him. Their fingers brushed and heat headed south to pool in Max's groin. There was a lot less room in his jeans suddenly.

Derek's cheeks flushed and those gorgeous blue eyes shot a quick glance down at the bulge in Max's pants. He wasn't embarrassed and didn't see the point in hiding his attraction to Derek.

"Max, I…"

He covered Derek's lips with one finger and smiled. "I'm not looking for forever, Derek. Only for one day at a time."

Derek sucked Max's finger into his mouth and stroked along the sides of it with his tongue.

"Fuck." Max tugged his finger away. "Can't talk to the men with a hard-on, Derek."

Max's heart jumped at the smooth sound of Derek's laugh.

"That would be rather uncomfortable. Should I make a lunch for us?"

Derek picked up his notebook and guitar, standing to head back inside. Max stared at Derek's ass covered in sweatpants, imagining what he looked like naked.

"Max, lunch?" Derek reminded him with a wicked twinkle in his eyes.

"No. I figured we'd ride over to Hardin's place and check on Peter." He shook his head, turning away from the tempting picture Derek made.

"Good idea. I was kind of worried about him." Derek nodded and disappeared inside.

"Get a grip on yourself, Furlo," Max muttered, strolling over to where his men were gathering. "Hard to work with a boner all day."

* * * *

Three hours later, Derek stood in one of the barns, eyeing the brown mare Max had led out for him. He rubbed her soft, inquisitive nose. Max set a saddle down on a rack next to them.

"She's gentle, Derek. I wouldn't put you on a horse you couldn't handle."

He closed his eyes as Max rubbed a hand over his shoulder. A warning sparked in his mind, saying he couldn't get lost in Max. The warning sounded remarkably like Thomas. His shoulders tensed and Max gave him a slight squeeze.

"Don't worry. No one here will talk. You're free to be who and what you want."

Derek nodded, understanding the freedom he'd been given.

"Thank you."

Max smiled and gave him a quick peck on the cheek. "You're welcome."

Gesturing to the saddle, Max asked, "Can you saddle Betsy?"

"It's been a while, but I think I can." He patted Betsy on the neck and reached for the saddle blanket.

"I'll check it when you're done."

He watched Max lead out a black and white gelding, hooking him into the cross-ties ahead of Betsy. Derek smoothed the blanket over Betsy's back to make sure there weren't any wrinkles before hefting the saddle up. He grabbed the girth, tightening it around Betsy's stomach. The stirrups were let down, but he didn't try adjusting them. He assumed Max would do that once Derek was mounted.

Betsy's bridle was next and the mare accepted the bit without a fuss. She mouthed it as Derek hooked the cheek straps.

"Ready?"

He turned to grin at Max. "I think so."

"Lead her out and I'll check."

Outside, he took the reins of Max's gelding and watched as Max tightened Betsy's girth again.

"Mount up and I'll adjust the stirrups for you."

Derek pushed up with his legs and settled into the wide leather Western saddle. Being used to the smaller English-style saddles, the Western one seemed huge. Shifting slightly, he decided he could get used to it.

"You're all set, except for this." Max held out a black cowboy hat.

"You would think that as a country singer, I would automatically wear a cowboy hat, but I only own ones I wear on stage."

He set it on his head and Max stroked his thigh. Derek's cock stiffened at the heat coming from Max's touch.

Max shot a look at Derek's groin and leered. "Just a little payback for this morning."

"You're not being very nice." Derek pouted.

Chuckling, Max strolled to where the gelding stood, reins hanging loose. Derek joined in. It had been a long time since he'd flirted and teased. He'd forgotten how stifling it was to stay in the closet.

He shook himself and told himself not to worry. For the time he stayed on the ranch, he would live as he wanted, not how the music execs ordered.

Max sat the gelding like he was part of the horse, adjusting to each shift of the horse's body. "Want to head out?"

"Yes." Derek meant yes to more than just the ride. He was ready for whatever this vacation gave him.

* * * *

Max and Derek rode into the yard at the Hardin ranch. A few of the hands waved as they went by.

"That's Hardin's housekeeper, Margie." Max nodded at the plump woman stepping out onto the front porch of the main house.

When they dismounted, Dave approached from one of the barns.

"Hey, Max. What brings you visiting?" Dave eyed Derek, but didn't say anything.

"I wanted to check on Peter. He stopped by yesterday and was pretty upset." He wasn't sure what—if anything—Peter might have told Dave.

"I would be too if my family decided to disown me. Luckily for me, my family's crazy enough not to care what I do, unless I kill someone."

Derek watched them with curious eyes. Max hesitated, not sure if Derek wanted anyone else to know who he was. Derek took it out of his hands by smiling and introducing himself.

"I'm Derek St Martin. I'm staying at the RM. Max was showing me around."

Recognition flared in Dave's eyes before he nodded.

"Nice to meet you, Mr St Martin. Hope you enjoy your stay." Dave gathered the reins and headed back towards the barn. "I'll take care of your horses. Call down to Barn Two when you're ready to go."

"Thanks, Dave."

Max gestured for Derek to follow him to the house.

"What does Dave do here?"

"He helps run Les' rough stock company. Dave and his dad manage the broncs. He used to ride and travel with Hersch. Got injured pretty badly in a wreck at a rodeo. He can't ride anymore because his back can't take the punishment."

"Another stray Master Leslie picked up." Margie gave Max a hug before turning to Derek. "I hope you found everything to your liking, Mr St Martin."

Derek flashed her the famous St Martin smile, but Max could see the sincerity in it.

"Everything is perfect, ma'am. Please call me Derek."

Max snorted. Randy had finally managed to get Margie to stop calling him Master Randy, and Les had accepted the fact Margie wouldn't call him anything else. It hadn't happened yet for any of the others. Max was certain Margie wasn't going to be so familiar with the country singer.

"If you need anything, let Max know and he'll make sure you get it."

She waved them inside and Derek shot Max an amused glance. He shrugged. There weren't words to describe Margie and her importance to Hardin's life.

"Is Peter here?"

Max hung his hat on a hook by the door and tugged off his boots. Derek followed his lead.

"Yes. He's in the study. Master Leslie called earlier to check up on him." Her knowing gaze met his. "He talked to you beforehand, right?"

He ducked his head. "I might have suggested Les call Peter. You know I don't talk about anyone else's business."

Margie patted his arm. "I know, dear. It was nice of you to do that. I think Peter is feeling better now. Why don't you go and see him? I have to start lunch. You'll stay, of course."

There wasn't any doubt in Margie's tone.

"Yes, ma'am."

They watched her leave. Derek bumped his shoulder as they went to the study.

"I have a feeling I know who runs this house."

"She's like everyone's mother. No one wants to disappoint or upset her. Hell, she's been with Hardin's family since before he was born. She helped raise him."

He knocked on the partially closed door.

"Come in," Peter called.

Pushing it open, he took in the mess of papers scattered over every possible surface. Peter's blond curls stood straight up like he'd been running his hands through them frequently.

"What the hell happened? Looks like a tornado hit." Max bent to pick up a pile off the end table.

"Don't touch those," Peter ordered. "I know where everything is. You'll screw up my system."

"Chaos is an organisational system now?" Derek joked. "Damn, the way my place in Nashville looks, I should be the most organised person in the world."

Max rolled his eyes but Peter laughed.

"It might not seem like it, but I really do have a system worked out here."

He wasn't going to question the kid. He grabbed Peter's wrist as he wandered by. Peter's gaze caught his with an absent-minded expression. Max figured Peter was burying himself in work so he wouldn't have to think about the family situation.

"It's time for lunch. Come help me entertain St Martin here." He jerked his head towards Derek who lounged in the doorway, watching them.

Peter flushed and stuttered, "I should really finish this."

"I don't know Hardin, but I bet he would rather you come eat with us than be cooped up in here all day."

Derek flashed another one of his famous smiles and Max watched Peter melt. He hid his own smile. So much charm. No wonder the man was one of the biggest stars in the country. Yet after watching Derek treat Peter and Margie like they were the stars — not him—Max had the feeling that polite and friendly person was closer to the real Derek than what they saw on stage.

* * * *

When lunch ended, Derek stood and started clearing the table. Margie protested and Derek interrupted her.

"You made a wonderful spread, ma'am. Cleaning up is the least I can do. You three go and relax. I'm perfectly capable of loading a dishwasher."

Max nodded, grabbed his iced tea and touched Peter on the arm. "Let's get before he changes his mind."

He caught the wink Derek sent his way. Derek was giving Peter and him a chance to talk without having a stranger listening in. Peter wandered ahead of him to the back porch.

After settling into one of the rocking chairs, he stretched his legs out before crossing his ankles. Peter sat on the top step and stared out towards the mountains.

"How you doing, kid?"

Peter shrugged. "Okay. It's weird, you know. I can't just run home to talk to Mom anymore."

"I understand, in a way. I had to get over wanting to call my mom every time something good happened to me. Mom died nine years ago."

"I'm sorry. Were you close?" Peter turned towards him.

As much as Max wanted to keep his past private, he didn't mind talking about his mom and he figured it would make Peter feel better.

"It was just my mom and me since I was born. She worked hard to give me what I needed. She was an artist as well, so we'd spend weekends painting or singing. We'd wander the Outback, hiking, and she taught me a lot I never learnt in school." He remembered the hours of fun he'd had with his mom.

"That must have been a great way to grow up," Peter commented.

"It was." He nudged Peter with the toe of his boot. "But maybe my loss isn't the same as yours. My mom didn't have a choice about leaving me."

Sadness and confusion welled in Peter's eyes. "I don't understand why they'd cut me out of their lives like that. It's not like I murdered someone or anything. I'm still their kid. Shouldn't they love me no matter what?"

"I don't know. I never met my father." Max heard the bitterness in his words.

"Some people should never be parents."

Both Max and Peter looked around. Derek stood just inside the door. Derek stepped out on the porch to rest his hip against the railing.

"My dad could care less about me. He and my mother divorced when I was five. He cut me out of his life as soon as the ink was dry on the papers. Mom married Eddie's father and I got a stepbrother." Derek picked at the paint on the wood. "It worked out best for us. We became our own family. There's nothing I wouldn't do for Eddie."

Max got up before crouching next to Peter to grip his shoulder. "That's the secret right there. It hurts your family turned from you, but there's a family right here, willing to welcome you with open arms."

Peter nodded. "You're right. Les said I was welcome to move in. There's more than enough room here."

"God knows, there's a ton of room here." He grimaced as he straightened. "Come on, St Martin. We need to finish checking the fence."

"Thanks for stopping by." Peter stood, hugging Max before offering Derek his hand with a shy smile. "I got the package you had sent, Mr St Martin. I'll take a look at it tonight."

Derek surprised both of them by pulling Peter in for a hug. "Be strong, Peter. It'll get easier."

Peter was speechless and Max shook his head.

"Call down to Barn Two and let Dave know we're ready to go."

"Sure, Max. Have a safe ride home." Peter headed back inside.

Max and Derek made their way down to Barn Two after collecting their hats.

"What exactly do Hardin and Hersch raise here?"

Derek studied all the ranch hands going about their business.

"A little of everything. Hersch breeds and trains cutting horses. Hardin runs a training facility for show jumpers and their riders."

A ranch hand brought out their horses, saddled and ready to go. Max made sure Derek mounted safely, with the added benefit of admiring the flex of Derek's ass in his faded jeans. When Derek was settled on Betsy, he swung into his saddle and led the way out of the yard.

"I thought Eddie told me Les didn't ride anymore."

Max bent down to unhook a gate. "He can't compete, but he can ride if he's careful. Hersch keeps an eye on him and just because he can't compete doesn't mean he doesn't know his stuff."

He let the gate swing open and gestured for Derek to ride through. After going through himself, he fastened it and they rode down the fence line.

"They also have a rough stock breeding programme. They're starting to contract with some of the rodeos in the area. Plus Hardin's the head of an international company."

Max thought about Les Hardin. The man was a multi-millionaire with fingers in so many pots, Max couldn't begin to keep them straight, but he always had time to help his friends out. Max knew Hardin considered him a friend, even though he'd never encouraged anything more than a working relationship with the man. If Max needed him, Hardin would do whatever was necessary to help him out.

"Les Hardin strikes me as a good guy. He was willing to let me stay when I needed to get away." Derek shifted.

Eyeing him, Max decided it was time to cut the riding short. He didn't want Derek so stiff he couldn't get out of bed tomorrow morning.

"Let's head back to the ranch. I have to work with some of the yearlings."

"Good idea. The break at lunch allowed my muscles to stiffen. I'd like to be able to walk without a limp."

They shared understanding grins and Max turned his gelding towards home. A stray thought crossed his mind.

Babysitting a celebrity was turning out to be easier than he thought.

Chapter Six

God, Derek was hungry. Riding out in all that fresh air had sparked his appetite. He pulled out pasta and a jar of homemade sauce. As he filled the pot with water, he started singing some phrases, testing them with the melody he had.

He grimaced as he stretched for the frozen garlic bread in the freezer. His muscles were a little sore from the exercise earlier. Stepping back, he ran into a solid body.

Strong hands gripped his waist. "Be careful. We don't want you hurting yourself."

Derek shivered as Max's warm breath washed over the nape of his neck. Before the thought actually registered in his brain, he pushed against Max and they groaned when his ass rubbed over Max's erection.

"I always thought you had a sweet ass," Max murmured in Derek's ear before nibbling on his neck.

"It's one of my best assets," he joked, covering Max's hands with his.

"Mmm…I can think of several of your assets I like."

He let Max turn him around and raised his chin, meeting Max's mouth. Their first kiss was gentle and slow, learning which angle gave them the most pleasure and how the other tasted.

Derek sucked on Max's tongue, letting go of Max's hands to bury his fingers in his hair. He pressed closer and enjoyed the feel of hard muscles and rough skin.

Fuck, it had been so long since he'd touched another in any way except casually. He could have found someone for a quick fuck, but he didn't like meaningless encounters. He liked sex, yet he wanted to know more about his lover than just a name.

Max bit Derek's bottom lip, soothing the sting with a quick swipe of his tongue. Derek whimpered as Max cupped his ass with his big hands and rocked their groins together.

A loud hiss pulled Derek's attention away from Max's mouth. He glanced at the stove and saw the water boiling over the edge of the pot. He thought about going and pouring the pasta in, but his legs weren't steady enough for him to move that far.

"I'll put the pasta in. You can get the garlic toast ready." Max grabbed the box of spaghetti and dumped it in the hot liquid.

"Turn the oven on," Derek said, opening the toast and placing them on a cookie sheet.

They made and consumed dinner in a companionable silence. Desire still simmered below the surface, making Derek's skin tingle each time Max brushed against him. He found he liked the slow build-up and anticipation of what would be coming next.

As they cleaned up, he realised he'd done most of the talking. Max had directed the conversation away from his own past and encouraged Derek to talk about his career.

"You don't like talking about yourself, do you?"

He nudged Max with his hip as they went into the living room and settled on the couch. Max grabbed the remote and turned on the TV before he answered. A baseball game was on.

"Not really. There's nothing exciting to tell. I lived in Sydney until I was twenty-two. After Mum died, I decided I needed a change, so I left and moved here. Did some rodeoing and working at other ranches. I started working for Romanos and MacCafferty two years ago." Max shrugged. "This is as good a place as any to stay for a while."

"And still that tells me nothing."

"Sorry, I'm just not good at conversation."

He shook his head. "Don't worry. I was only kidding."

Max encircled Derek's shoulders, bringing him closer to him. Derek rested his head on Max's chest and listened to his heartbeat. There was something far more intimate in cuddling on the couch than lying naked in a bed. It resembled an actual relationship, instead of just fucking.

The steady in-and-out of Max's breathing relaxed Derek and he found himself blinking, trying to stay awake. Max rearranged them, so they were lying on the couch, his back to Max's chest and arms wrapped around his waist. The heat of Max's body seeped into Derek's and he fell asleep, trusting Max to keep him safe.

Derek woke with a jolt when Max eased from behind him. Crouching down beside the couch, Max ran his hand over Derek's hair.

"Hush, honey. I have to go sleep in a real bed or I'll be stiffer than a board tomorrow. Why don't you move to your bedroom?"

He moaned as Max cupped his cheek and whispered a kiss over his lips. "I don't sleep much. I'll probably stay up and see if I can get some more songs written."

"I don't sleep well either and I don't think that'll change now that I know what it's like to have you in my arms," Max admitted.

Derek decided to take a leap. The worst that could happen was Max said no. Sitting up, he ran a hand through his hair and sighed.

"What do you say to sharing your bed with me? I don't toss and turn. At least I don't think I do. Never shared a bed with anyone to know for sure." He blushed slightly.

"Really? What about all those ladies the tabloids have tied you to?"

"Just cover, man. You know that. I don't go for girls and never have. It made my manager happy to get me an escort to the awards shows and shit like that."

Max stood, his knees creaking, and held out his hand. "Go grab your toothbrush and some sweats if you want to wear them. I usually sleep naked, but I'll put shorts on if it'll bother you."

Naked Max? No way was Derek going to say no to that. He smiled. "I don't mind naked."

Going upstairs, he grabbed his toothbrush, guitar and notebook. He wasn't sure he'd be able to sleep, even in Max's arms, so he wanted to be prepared to write.

When he got back downstairs, Max had shut off the TV and the lights. He waited for Derek by the back door. They slipped on their boots before heading out to Max's house.

Derek didn't really look around as they headed upstairs. Nervousness hit him as he entered Max's bedroom.

He'd never gone to a person's bed with the express purpose of actually sleeping. Come to think of it, he'd never gone to anyone's personal bed. For eight years he'd been celibate and before that, any kind of encounter he had was in the back alley or the bathroom of whatever bar he'd been playing in.

After setting down his guitar in the corner and his notebook on the dresser, he turned to see Max standing in the doorway with a smile on his face.

"A little weird, huh?" The cowboy gestured to the door across the hall. "The bath's there and I laid out some clean towels if you wanted to take a shower tonight."

"Just slightly. I'll brush my teeth and be right back."

He took care of getting ready for bed and returned to find the lights were off. Max was in bed already and Derek couldn't help saying a silent thank you to the man.

God, it shouldn't be this awkward. He stripped and climbed under the blankets. Max rolled over on his side, throwing an arm over Derek's waist and pulling him closer.

"Is this okay?" Max whispered against his ear.

How could he say no? Max's embrace cradled him tight to the man's warm firm body and Derek rested his head on Max's shoulder.

"It's perfect," he murmured.

A soft snore answered his statement and he laughed softly.

* * * *

Max slapped his alarm clock, silencing the annoying buzz. He stretched and frowned when his hand landed on the empty space next to him. Turning his head, he glanced around. Derek wasn't in the room.

Sniffing, he smiled as he climbed out of bed. Derek had made coffee at some point. After showering, he went downstairs and glanced in his living room on his way to the kitchen.

Derek was curled up in the corner of Max's couch, guitar in his arms and notebook resting on the back of the couch. He strummed a few cords, holding a pencil between his teeth.

Max strolled over and touched Derek's hair, threading his fingers through the man's dark curls. Derek leaned his head back and grinned, taking the pencil out of his mouth.

"Hey there." Max bent and kissed him quick.

"Mmmm…" Derek sighed and slid a hand up to cup Max's cheek for a moment before easing away. "Good morning. I made coffee."

"I smell it. Thanks." Max continued on to the kitchen. "You want some?"

"Sure. I can always use the caffeine. Just black, please." Derek scribbled something down.

After taking two mugs out, Max poured the steaming liquid into them. He took Derek's to the man before going back and getting the bread to make some toast.

"You want toast, Derek?" he called.

"Sure."

Max got the toast made and put on some plates while listening to Derek sing softly. Carrying the food, he stopped in the doorway and grinned.

The singer frowned as he played and sang. He didn't seem to notice Max setting the plate on the coffee table. Max took the other end of the couch, devouring two pieces before Derek looked up and blinked.

"Oh, hey."

Laughing, he gestured to the food. "Your toast is a little cold, but it's here."

Derek picked one up and took a bite. "That's okay," he said after swallowing. "I'm used to my food getting cold while I write."

"Whatever you're working on sounds good." He rested his head on the back of the couch, cradling his cup to his stomach.

"It needs something." Derek shrugged. "I'll figure it out eventually."

Max wrapped a hand around Derek's ankle, running his fingers up and down the skin under the hem of Derek's jeans.

"Did you sleep at all?" he asked.

"A few hours. No big deal. I got enough rest when I first got off tour. I was really wiped out. When I'm feeling good, I don't need much." Derek closed his eyes and stretched out his legs, placing them in Max's lap.

"I'm the same way." He massaged those long feet and trailed his finger along the arch of Derek's foot.

Derek twitched and laughed. "Stop."

"Oh, someone's ticklish."

Max moved his mug out of harm's way before he pinned Derek to the couch and started digging his fingers into the man's side.

"Stop," Derek gasped, flailing around and struggling to flip Max off him. "Bastard."

He kept up until Derek stopped flopping and threw his hands above his head, smooth, tanned chest heaving. Max was tempted to pinch those dark brown nipples and lick them.

"Uncle. I give up." Derek was laughing so hard he couldn't fight anymore.

"Okay." Max placed a quick peck on the tip of the man's nose before standing up and offering Derek his hand. "I have to get dressed and hand out assignments to the men. You want to meet back here around ten for a real breakfast?"

Derek studied him for a moment, running his gaze over Max's body, stopping at the noticeable lump in Max's jeans. A wicked gleam came in the singer's eyes and Max stepped back.

"Don't even think about it."

He wasn't fast enough. Derek pushed up on his knees to press his face to Max's groin. Groaning, Max buried his hands in Derek's hair while arching his hips. Hot, moist air penetrated his jeans and underwear, bathing his cock in sensations guaranteed to make him hard all day if he didn't get that mouth wrapped around him at some point.

Derek broke his hold with ease and stood. "Sure. I'll make pancakes."

Gripping the man's shoulder, Max jerked him to his chest. He covered that wicked mouth with his and kissed the singer until Derek melted against him, encircling his waist with his arms.

They broke apart when Max's lungs screamed for oxygen. Derek stared at him in shocked surprise, lust burning in those blue eyes.

"You're a bit of a tease, aren't you?" Max adjusted himself, trying to find room in his suddenly too-tight jeans.

Derek shrugged. "You have to learn how to flirt. Drives the fans crazy. I'd never tease you though. I'll always put out for you."

"That's good to know. Pancakes sound good to me." He left Derek gathering up the plates and mugs.

Coming back downstairs, he brushed another kiss over Derek's cheek as the singer rinsed out their mugs. "You can stay here if you want. I'm not kicking you out or anything."

"Won't your men think we slept together?"

"We did sleep together," he teased. "Actually, I've never hidden the fact I'm gay, just never talked about it either. The men who work here know the rules. No matter what they think, they don't work here if they can't keep their opinions to themselves."

He pulled on his boots and grabbed a jacket. It might be summer, but early mornings could still be chilly in Wyoming. "The bosses make it clear to every hand who hires on here."

Derek laughed. "I can't see any of them talking back to MacCafferty."

"They don't, but he isn't the one they need to worry about. Romanos is by far the leader on the ranch." Pushing open the back door, he smiled at Derek.

Derek waved at him. "Get going. The stock won't feed themselves."

Max left and for the first time greeted his men with a grin instead of a grunt.

Chapter Seven

Derek sat under the oak, watching Max work with a young filly. She fidgeted and shied away each time he reached for her, but Max stayed calm. His voice stayed low and no hint of frustration showed in it. In fact, he crooned so softly that the filly had to strain to hear him and Derek realised that was what Max wanted. He used her natural curiosity to encourage her to accept his touch.

He scribbled a line or two down in the notebook resting on his knee before glancing back up at the other man. In the week since they admitted their attraction to each other, Derek had discovered he enjoyed these moments as much as he did the make-out sessions. They hadn't done anything more than a little petting and rubbing off. No actual sex yet and it was strange for him. At one time, he'd been all about the sex, but it was nice to take it slow and get to know someone before they had sex. Max didn't seem in any more of a hurry than he did.

"There you go, pretty girl. See, this blanket isn't going to hurt you." Max bent and picked up a saddle blanket, holding it so the filly could see it.

Derek tried not to shift, but looking at Max's tight ass encased in those faded jeans made his mouth water and his cock hard. Necking, petting and heavy breathing was all well and good, but he was ready to move their relationship to the next level.

Also, Max had informed him earlier that Romanos and MacCafferty would be returning in a couple of days. As strange as it sounded, even to him, Derek didn't want their first time to be when there were other people around. He would get questions anyway, since he'd moved his stuff from the big house into Max's place two days ago.

"You ready to head in? It's almost dinnertime."

He glanced up to see Max holding out a hand to help him up. He took it, moving slowly so he didn't startle the filly. Reaching up, he cupped his hand around the back of Max's head and kissed him.

"After dinner, we should talk," he said when he pulled away.

Max frowned. "Sounds sort of ominous."

"Nothing bad. Trust me." He gathered his notebook and tucked it in his backpack. "I'll meet you back at your place. The roast should be done cooking and I'll make some biscuits up."

"To look at you, no one would know you were so domesticated." Max laughed as Derek swatted his ass.

He watched Max lead the filly back to one of the barns. It was only after Max had disappeared into the building that Derek moved to head to Max's house. He set his pack on the floor next to the back door and pulled off his boots.

Padding into the kitchen in his socks, he glanced at the crockpot. The scents floating from it played with his nose and he sniffed in appreciation. The roast smelt delicious. Now it was time to make biscuits. He washed his hands before gathering all the ingredients.

By the time Max came in, the biscuits were finishing up in the oven and he'd got the roast out and cut. He grinned at Max's hum of contentment.

"Nothing says home more than walking into a warm kitchen filled with delicious smells." Max gave him a quick peck. "Do I have time for a quick shower before dinner?"

"Sure. The biscuits are almost done, but I can keep them warm until you come back down."

"Thanks."

He wanted to offer to join Max in the shower, but figured he needed to clear the air before they had sex.

Ten minutes later, Max strolled into the kitchen and sat at the table where Derek set the food and drinks. After they'd eaten a few bites, Max glanced at Derek with a smile.

"Are you going to tell me what you wanted to talk about now or do I have to suffer in curiosity until after dinner?"

Derek fidgeted with his fork for a second then sighed. "I just wanted you to know that I haven't had sex with a guy for eight years."

"I know. You told me earlier. That's why we agreed to go slow." Max frowned.

"I have had sex with women during that time."

Max set his silverware down slowly and leant back in his chair. "So you're telling me you're bi?"

"Not really." He shrugged. "Well, yes, I guess I could be considered bi. I've had sex with women before, but it doesn't ring my bell like fucking a guy does."

"I'm not sure I completely understand. Explain this all to me." Max folded his arms over his chest and levelled a steady gaze on Derek.

"I promised my agent I wouldn't mess around with guys. He said it wasn't good for my career." He abandoned his dinner and stood before pacing around the kitchen. "I dated girls as cover. I couldn't go to an award ceremony stag, you know, but I also couldn't take anyone I really wanted with me. Some of those girls over the years wound up in my bed because I was lonely and horny."

Max pursed his lips as he thought for a moment. "None of your band members knew or suspected you might be gay?"

He shook his head. "I never met any of those guys until after I signed my first recording contract. After that, it was easy to hide from them. They didn't really care what I did as long as they were still playing music and making money. They'd see girls leave my hotel room at all hours of the night and congratulate me the next day on being a stud. I didn't feel like telling them the truth."

Bracing his hands on the edge of the sink, he stared out of the window. "I know that makes me a terrible person. I used those girls and lied to everyone."

He jumped when Max embraced him from behind, drawing him back against Max's chest.

Max nuzzled behind Derek's ear and nibbled on his earlobe before saying, "It doesn't make you a terrible person. It just makes you human. You were searching for a way not to be lonely. Did you ever promise those girls anything other than one night?"

"No. To be honest, I felt dirty and ended up taking scalding showers every time I slept with one of them." He shuddered.

"Why didn't you hire someone?" Max licked a line from behind Derek's ear down to where his shirt gaped open and revealed his collarbone.

Derek shook his head slightly. "Couldn't risk it. There was too much danger that one of them would get an offer he couldn't refuse and tell some tabloid all about the night he spent with Derek St Martin."

"Hmmm…you were probably right not to do that."

He turned to face Max. "Why aren't you more upset about this? I thought you'd throw a fit."

Max stepped back, a puzzled frown on his face. "Throw a fit? First of all, I'm not the type of guy who throws fits and second of all, you did what you did to survive. I'm not going to judge you for that."

Smiling, he cupped Max's face and brushed a kiss over the man's lips. "Thank you."

Max grinned before moving towards the table. "Let's clean up here. We can make coffee and watch some TV before we head to bed."

"Ummm…" His cheeks heated and his tongue didn't seem to want to work. "I was thinking maybe we could go to bed sooner rather than later."

Pausing in mid-stride, Max glanced at him with a warm leer. "Are you suggesting…?"

Derek nodded and cursed himself for acting like a virgin. God, he'd been with lovers before. Admittedly just women in the past couple of years, but still it wasn't like he'd never had sex before in his life.

Max set the plates he carried in the sink and grabbed Derek's hand. "Come on. Don't be shy now."

Laughing, he let Max drag him up the stairs to his bedroom. It would be okay. They could take their time and he trusted Max not to rush things.

"Get naked," Max ordered while heading for the nightstand by the bed.

Derek pulled his shirt over his head before tossing it to the side. He reached for the button on his shorts when Max shouted in triumph and turned, holding up a bottle of lube and several foil packages.

"Good to know you're prepared. I didn't think I'd find an opportunity here in cowboy country to get any, so I didn't pack supplies." He winked and Max laughed.

"Always be prepared is my motto. Now let me help you with those."

Max tossed the condoms and lube on the bed before kneeling in front of Derek and sliding his fingers under his waistband.

Derek sucked in his stomach, giving Max more room. He combed his fingers through Max's hair, enjoying the feel of the soft curls catching on his calluses. He trembled as Max trailed his own fingers down into the hair around the base of his cock.

"Oh," he gasped as Max tugged on them.

Max slipped his hand down to cup Derek's cock as he pulled the zipper down, protecting his erection. Derek wiggled slightly, and with a little shove from Max, his shorts fell to his ankles. He braced his hands on Max's shoulders and stepped out of them.

Kicking them out of the way, he moaned when Max licked the wet tip of his cock.

"I won't last," he warned. "It's been too long."

Too long since he'd felt the firm grip of a man's hand.

Max looked up at him with a grin. "That's all right. We get you off fast the first time, you'll last longer the next time around."

His words did nothing to ease Derek's building climax. Max brought the flared head of Derek's cock to his mouth and started to suck it in.

"Wait."

Heaving a frustrated sigh, Max rocked back on his heels and looked at him in expectation. "Yes?"

He blushed slightly, but went on. "You should use a rubber. I haven't been tested for at least a year, Max. I was careful when I fucked the women, but before that, when I was young and crazy, I wasn't so safe."

Max frowned. "Were you clean the last time you were tested?"

"Yes, but you shouldn't take my word on it. I mean I wouldn't hurt you for the world. I just don't want to risk it."

"I don't really like the taste of latex," Max murmured.

Derek touched the top of Max's head. "I know. Neither do I, but it's better to be safe than sorry."

He thought about suggesting tests, but decided that asking that would move their fling to something far more serious and it wasn't time for that yet. There might never be the right time for that sort of commitment.

Max grunted as he got to his feet. "Come lie on the bed. My knees are too old to be kneeling on the floor for long."

Relief shot through Derek and he rushed to climb up on the mattress. Leaning back against the pillows, he spread his legs for Max to lie between. The crinkling of foil drew his attention and he glanced down to watch Max tear open the packet.

Flashing him a wicked wink, Max placed the rubber on the tip of Derek's dick before leaning forward and using his mouth to roll the condom down the length of Derek's shaft.

"Oh my God," Derek breathed, his head falling back and hitting the headboard.

Max relaxed his throat, taking Derek's cock in until it hit the back. He pinned the singer's slender hips to the mattress, so he could get used to the fullness. Derek slipped his hands through Max's hair, but didn't do anything except stroke.

He swallowed around Derek before pulling back until only the tip rested in his mouth. Holding the head gently in his teeth, he flicked the spongy flesh, wishing he could suck Derek bare. Nothing beat the taste of sweat dancing on his tongue and the taste of latex tended to make him want to gag, but he would be safe for Derek.

Sliding down on his stomach, Max licked down the throbbing vein along the underside until he reached Derek's lightly furred balls. He drew one in and sucked hard, applying enough suction to make Derek cry out.

"Fuck, Max. What are you trying to do to me?"

He pulled away with a slight pop and grinned at Derek's protest. "If you can still talk in complete sentences, I haven't accomplished what I planned on."

Keeping one hand on Derek's balls, massaging and tugging on them, Max wrapped his other hand around the base of Derek's shaft and took the man in again. He lowered his head until his lips touched the top of his hand. Moving his hand and head in unison, he blew Derek while jacking him off as well.

His spit eased the friction and soon Derek was moaning, moving his hips slightly, obviously not wanting to overwhelm him. Max nodded his head, humming to let Derek know he could move faster and shove further in. Letting go of Derek's dick, he gripped the singer's hips with both hands and encouraged Derek to thrust.

"Ah," Derek called. He buried his hand in Max's hair and tugged with each withdrawal.

The man moved faster and faster. Soon all Max could do was make sure his muscles were relaxed and somehow manage to breathe while Derek fucked him.

"Max, I'm gonna…" Derek grunted, taking a tight grip on Max's hair, and pushed until the head hit the back of Max's throat.

He swallowed around his lover's shaft and warmth filled the condom. Derek's hips jerked a few times before he slumped back against the pillows, his hold eased and turned into petting. Max leant back, allowing Derek's softening dick to slip from his mouth. He lay on his back, staring up at the ceiling and catching his breath.

"Are you okay?" Derek asked.

"I'm fine. Just give me a second." Reaching out, he stroked his fingers along the groove between hip and abs.

"Good, because I don't think I'll be able to move any time soon."

They chuckled as Max pushed himself off the bed before heading to the bathroom to grab some toilet paper. He returned, took care of the condom and cleaned Derek off. The entire time Derek watched him, not saying anything.

After tossing the paper and condom into the wastebasket next to the bed, he grabbed another rubber and rolled it on his own erection. He ached to pound Derek's ass, but he knew he needed to take his time getting the man ready for his cock.

He reached for the lube and popped the top, squirting some on his fingers. While he did that, Derek slipped his hands behind his knees and spread them back and to the side, exposing his hole to Max.

"So hot," he murmured, running along Derek's crease to where the puckered flesh hid.

Tapping it softly, he grinned as Derek groaned.

"You like that, huh? You'll love this, I bet."

Max pressed his finger into Derek, not stopping until it was buried as far as it could go. He rubbed his hand over the singer's stomach, soothing the man while he adjusted to being invaded. Within a few seconds, his lover relaxed and squeezed his muscles around him. That was the sign he was looking for.

Removing his finger, he poured a little more slick before easing two back in.

"Oh, fuck," Derek moaned, his hips lifting off the bed and he thrashed his head from side to side.

"Too much?"

"No, just give me a second."

They had all the time in the world as far as Max was concerned. He slid his free hand up Derek's chest to pinch lightly at the man's nipples, distracting him a little from the pressure in his ass. Twisting and flicking hardened those little pieces of flesh and caused Derek's dick to stiffen as well.

"Are you ready for more?"

Derek nodded, pushing like he wanted to take more of Max inside, and he lost his patience. Jerking out, he poured lube onto the palm of his hand and coated his cock with it. He hooked his arms around Derek's legs and positioned the flared head of his dick at Derek's opening.

"Try to relax and push out. I'll go slow."

Derek nodded and bit his lip as Max started pressing in, taking his time, but not stopping until his thighs hit firm ass cheeks. He dropped Derek's legs, falling forward to brace his arms on either side of Derek's head.

"Are you okay?"

Eyes screwed shut and teeth clenched, Derek shrugged. "I just need a minute."

"Honey, now that I'm where I wanted to be since the day I met you, I'm not in any hurry to leave."

Surging up, Derek crushed their lips together and that movement drove Max deep enough to hit the man's prostrate. The dark-haired man tore their kiss apart and yelled. "Fuck."

Max leered. "I think you're ready now."

He pulled out until just the tip of his shaft remained inside the ring of muscle. Derek reached out and wrapped his hands around the wrought-iron bars of Max's headboard. With a short nod, he tilted his hips and encouraged Max to take him.

Free of worry about hurting Derek, he slammed back in and drove a grunt from his lover. The slapping of flesh hitting flesh filled the room as he rode Derek's ass fast and hard, forcing them closer and closer to their mutual climaxes.

"Good… Full… Amazing."

It seemed his singer was a bit of a babbler when he got fucked. Max couldn't say anything. His brain was slowly melting as pressure pooled under his skin and his cock swelled. He did his best to nail Derek's gland with each thrust, wanting the singer to come along with him when he shot over the edge.

Prising his hand from the sheet it twisted, he wrapped it around Derek's length and let his own motion drive Derek's shaft through the tunnel his fingers created. Max gripped tighter as the pre-cum dripping from Derek eased the friction a little.

"Gonna come soon," he warned.

"Go ahead," Derek panted. "I'll be right with you."

Max flung his head back and yelled as his climax rose through him. He filled the rubber he wore with each spurt. Derek cried out as well, his ass clamping down, and with each spasm, he milked every drop he could from Max.

When Max's mind began to function again, he fell to the side of Derek, careful about the condom. He got it off without too much mess, threw it in the basket and wiped them both clean with one of the T-shirts he'd left lying on the floor.

"We should take a shower," Derek mumbled as he snuggled closer, laying his head on Max's chest.

"After a nap."

He buried his nose in Derek's sweat-dampened curls and breathed in deep of the scents he loved. Sweat, sex, and all male. It might hurt in the end when Derek returned to Nashville, but Max was willing to take what he could get and regret it later, instead of regretting never taking a chance at all.

Chapter Eight

A truck door slamming woke Derek. He stretched and reached out to where Max would have been sleeping. Coming up empty, he rolled over to check the clock. Almost nine in the morning. His lover would have been out of bed by five, no matter how little sleep he'd got from their activities the night before.

Derek grinned and slid from the bed. It had been three days since the first time they'd made love and every night ended with them in bed, fucking and loving. They were the best nights of rest Derek had had in years.

He tugged on a pair of sweat pants before wandering over to the window. A dark green crew cab truck was parked in front of the main house and three men stood talking beside it. Derek knew one of the men was Max. He'd recognise that body and stance anywhere.

Pulling a T-shirt from a pile of clean clothes, he put it on as he made his way down the stairs and headed towards the back door where he found his tennis shoes. He slipped them on before he peered out of the small window beside the door.

Now that he was closer, he recognised Brody McCafferty, his former bodyguard. A sigh forced itself from his chest. Max's bosses were home and things would change.

He pushed open the door and stood on the porch, watching Max help the other two men unload their truck. Romanos and MacCafferty were opposites in appearance. MacCafferty was tall and blond while Romanos was on the shorter side, stocky and dark-haired.

Something told him their personalities would be different as well, with Romanos being the more outgoing of the two. Yet the way they moved together and touched spoke of a deeper connection.

They joked and slapped Max's back in greeting.

"Where is our houseguest? You didn't scare him off, did you?" Romanos winked at MacCafferty.

"No."

Derek grimaced when Max turned and gestured for him to join them. Time for his romantic summer fling to end and for him to crash head-first into reality.

As he sauntered closer, all three men watched him. MacCafferty and Romanos studied him appraisingly, like they were calculating how much trouble he was going to be, but it was Max's gaze that burned into his chest and stiffened his cock.

"Mr Romanos. Brody." He offered his hand. "It was nice of you to let me stay here while you were gone."

Tony grinned. "Call me Tony. I never thought I'd see you again after the plane ride we took together."

Derek peered closer at those laughing dark eyes and bright grin. A memory of seeing that face before shot through his mind and he remembered one episode, two years ago, when he'd broken away from his handlers and caught a commercial flight to San Francisco from Hawaii.

He'd sat next to a bull rider, heading home as well. They'd flirted with each other and talked. It had been one of the most relaxing moments Derek had had in a long time. The bull rider's face had faded around the edges a little, but he still remembered the grin.

"I'll be damned. That's why your name sounded familiar when Max mentioned you."

Forgetting himself, he hugged Tony tight.

"Congratulations on winning the championship the next year. I got so caught up in my tour that I wasn't able to follow you last year. How did you do?"

"If I was a jealous man, I'd be worried that you two shared more than a plane ride together," Brody teased as he gestured for Max to grab two of the bags.

"There are a few things you can do in first class during a plane ride, but I wasn't about to blow my cover."

"I'll have to ask you about them. Brody and I take a lot of flights during the season." Tony leered at the blond.

Max chuckled and his bosses stopped to stare at him. Derek saw his lover blush and duck his head.

"What's so interesting?" Max mumbled.

"I don't think I've ever heard you laugh," Brody pointed out.

Derek could tell Max was feeling uncomfortable, so he drew their attention to him.

"Where are you two coming home from?"

"We were in Germany. My nephew competed in a horse show over there and I had a break from the tour, so we all flew over to support him."

Tony dropped his bags at the foot of the stairs and wandered back towards the kitchen.

"You all want some coffee?" he called.

"There's nothing made over here."

Brody's bags joined Tony's before the blond turned to study Derek and Max. Both of them shifted under that knowing gaze, but Brody didn't say anything about what he was thinking.

"Tony will get the coffee started. I'm starving. How about you two join us for some breakfast?"

"Yes, sir."

Derek nodded. They made their way back and found Tony dragging out pans. Brody joined in while waving Max and Derek to take seats at the breakfast table. Under the noise of the couple fixing the food, Derek leaned over and bumped Max with his shoulder.

"This is a little awkward, isn't it?" he spoke under his breath.

"They don't mean to make you uncomfortable," Max said. "They just aren't used to seeing me with anyone."

"How do they know we're a couple?"

"The same way every other couple knows. We must give off pheromones or glow in that special way. Plus, you're wearing one of my shirts and came out of my house."

He glanced down at the T-shirt he wore. It had Sydney screen-printed across the front.

"How do they know I don't have one of these? I did a tour in Australia one year."

"They've seen that particular shirt before."

Dropping his hand under the table, he rubbed Max's knee.

"Do you want to cool it for a while?"

It hurt more than he thought it would to ask, but he was ready to step back if that was what Max wanted. Hell, he knew all about wanting privacy.

Max shot him a surprised glance. "Cool it? Hell no. We'll just need to adjust to the fact that they're here now."

"Not for long."

They jumped apart and swung to see Brody standing by the table with plates in his hands. He grinned at their sheepish looks, but didn't comment on the fact that Derek's hand was still under the table. After setting down the plates, he took the silverware and glasses from Tony.

"The tour starts up next week, so Tony's heading out for that and I have some meetings in Los Angeles with Vance and Morgan. This is just a quick stopover to make sure everything's running smooth here and grab clean clothes."

"Where are you at in the standings, Tony?"

Derek poured coffee for everyone. They all filled their plates and started to eat.

"I'm in third. Last year was rough. I had a few injuries that just wouldn't heal."

"They would have healed fine if you had taken time to let them," Brody pointed out.

The way Tony rolled his eyes told Derek it was a long-standing argument. He dipped his head to hide his smile and Max caught his gaze with a wink.

"I had to rehab hard over the off season to get back to where I was when I won the championship. It took a couple of events, but I'm finally feeling the rhythm again. Some of the other guys are really stepping up this year."

"They all want to beat the best, I bet."

Derek knew how that was. All the new young singers wanted to knock him out of the top spot. He used to worry about that and losing his fans to some other young fool with a tight ass and a great voice. After his last tour, he couldn't muster up the energy to fret about it anymore. As he lay in his bed, drugged to the gills and watching the ceiling swirl around above him, he had decided it wasn't worth it.

He'd continue to put out the best music he could and hope that his fans kept buying it. If not, it wasn't like he didn't have enough money to survive without touring or putting another album out.

"Where'd you leave Yancey?" Max pushed his empty plate away and grabbed his coffee.

"In Cheyenne. His summer classes start in two days and he isn't in the greatest of moods." Brody shook his head. "Hard to say goodbye to the man you love when you know you won't be seeing him for a long time."

"Juan stay in Germany?"

"Yeah. His trainer wants him to get some international experience, so he'll be riding throughout Europe with his barn. One of the best things Les ever did for us was convincing Merrill to take Juan on as a rider." Tony shook his head. "I never thought one of my family would be into that fancy English riding."

"But he's good at it, or Les would never have offered to sponsor him." Brody stood, gathered some plates and carried them to the sink.

"True." Tony shot a look at Max. "How have things been going since we left?"

Derek climbed to his feet and smiled. "That's when I head out. I'm going to shower and get dressed. Is it all right if I take Betsy out to that creek we saw on our ride yesterday? I'll be careful."

Max nodded and Derek barely managed to keep from kissing him. That easy familiarity would have to take a back seat when Max's bosses were around. He didn't want them thinking he was distracting the man from his job.

"Will you join us for dinner tonight, Derek?" Brody asked. "Les and Randy are coming over. We're going to cook out."

"I'd love to. Thanks."

He smiled at the three of them and left. By leaving, it also gave them time to question Max about what was going on between them. Not that either of them really knew.

Max stared into his coffee mug, silently cursing his lover for leaving him to the tender mercies of his bosses. He knew both men were bursting to ask him what was going on between him and Derek. God, they were worse than a bunch of old women gossiping over the back fence. When the door shutting signalled Derek had left the house, Brody and Tony whirled to look at him.

"What?" he mumbled, unable to meet their incredulous gazes.

"Are you sleeping with Derek St Martin?"

The shock in Tony's voice made Max tense.

"Not that it's any of your business, but what if I am?"

"The man considered country music's sexiest? The man that everyone thinks is straight?"

He shrugged. "You're not telling me anything I don't already know."

"You know that he'll have to go back to Nashville at some point, right?" Brody's question was softer and filled with concern.

"I know that. I'm not stupid, okay? I went into this whole thing with my eyes wide open. I appreciate your concern, but it's my choice." He stood and set the cup on the table. "Is that all, or do you really want to know what has gone on with the ranch while you were gone?"

"Oh sit down, Max," Tony ordered him. "You know we do this because we care. It doesn't matter if it's you or any of our friends. We just don't want to see you hurt."

Max sat, pushing his mug across the table. "It's going to hurt. There's no way to avoid it, but I'd rather go into this, knowing that, than think there's a possibility of something more between us."

Brody joined him at the table. "I have to say this. I don't know if it's you or being away from the music world, but Derek's never looked so good and relaxed. When I worked for him, he was strung tighter than barbed wire. Drugs kept him going and it got to the point where he was so brittle, I thought the wrong word or touch would shatter him."

"He was like that when I met him," Tony said quietly. "It's rough when a man's dream beats him down to the point where he needs help to keep going."

"Derek's doing better. He's not living on that crap anymore. The worst he does is a beer or two at night and cigarettes."

Max couldn't believe he was talking about his lover behind his back. Straightening in his chair, he met Brody and Tony's gazes.

"Here's what you need to know about the ranch."

His bosses realised the subject of Derek was closed for now.

* * * *

After they finished their discussion, Brody and Tony went up to unpack and Max wandered out to the barns, checking on the stock and his men. Everything was running smoothly and he stared out towards the oak tree where he knew Derek would be.

There were plenty of things that needed Max's attention, but he found himself saddling up his gelding and riding towards the creek. He wanted to make sure Derek wasn't upset with the obvious fact they were going to talk about him after he left.

Betsy was grazing and Max was glad to see Derek had removed her bridle, replacing it with a halter and a lead rope like Max had taught him. The mare nickered softly when she saw them ride up. After swinging down, he ground-hitched his mount then strolled towards the creek.

Derek stood in the middle of the water, his feet bare and his jeans rolled up to keep from getting wet. Max wasn't sure what his lover was doing as Derek stared down into the running water, muttering to himself.

"What are you doing?"

Jerking upright, Derek lost his balance. His arms flailing, he tried to right himself, but he couldn't and fell ass-first into the water. The look of shock on his face caused Max to double over and laugh, holding his stomach and wiping tears from his face.

"Oh, you think you're funny, huh?"

That was the only warning he got before two clammy hands grasped his arms and yanked him into the water.

"Fuck," he yelled. His hat went flying as he scrambled back towards the bank. "That's fucking cold."

"Of course it is, jackass."

He flopped onto the grass and stared up at Derek, who stood above him, dripping wet.

"Why were you standing in the middle of it then?"

He asked, but he wasn't as interested as he should have been in the answer. Derek's T-shirt was plastered to him, showing every dip and cut of the man's chest and abs, along with a hint of hair dusting his skin. The cold liquid pebbled Derek's nipples and Max wanted to wrap his lips around those little nubs of flesh. His gaze trailed down to where the soaked denim cradled Derek's cock, which didn't seem affected by the dunking its owner had received.

"You should take those wet clothes off. We don't want you to get a cold," he suggested, his voice husky with desire.

Derek eyed him. "I'm sure my health is the first thought on your mind."

He tried to look innocent, but he couldn't drag his gaze from the growing bulge in the singer's jeans.

"You wound me." He pouted, reaching out to tug on Derek's jeans. "I really don't want you to get sick."

"So wet country singers get you hot, huh?"

Derek stripped the T-shirt off first, letting the soggy fabric hit Max in the face when he dropped it.

"Only if it's you."

Sitting up, Max tore off his own shirt, thanking God that he wore one with snaps instead of buttons. He flung it to the side seconds before Derek straddled him and pushed him back.

"Oomph…"

Derek followed him down and crushed their lips together. He speared his fingers through those brown curls he loved to touch. He duelled with Derek over who would control the kiss, but when Derek bit his bottom lip hard, he yielded.

While he sucked on Derek's tongue, which had swept in to tease his, he rocked his hips up against Derek's groin.

He tore his mouth away and swore, "Shit. I want you to fuck me."

Derek shook his head. "Can't. No condoms or lube."

"Fuck. Guess maybe I need to start packing those in my saddlebags then," he joked.

"It's all right."

He trailed his hands over Derek's shoulders and down his chest to twist those nipples when Derek reared up on his knees. Devouring his lover with his gaze, he watched the man struggle to open his jeans and push the sides out of the way as his cock sprang free of its confinement. He sucked in his breath at the sight of that thick length. He really wanted to feel Derek riding him with it, but that would have to wait.

"Hey."

"Ouch." Max rubbed his chest where Derek had pinched him. "What?"

"Help me get yours out and then we can have a little fun."

His eyes lit up. There wouldn't be any fucking or sucking, but there could be some jerking and rubbing. They would both be able to come and he'd be able to ride fence without causing serious injury to himself.

Fumbling together, they managed to uncover his shaft then sighed as their heated flesh brushed against each other. He wrapped his hand around their erections and Derek joined him, stroking hard and fast.

"Oh, God," Derek cried out.

Max pumped the way he liked it, with a little twist of his palm over the heads, gathering the pre-cum pooling there. Somehow, Derek bent to kiss him without breaking their connection. He tasted the coffee and bacon the singer had had for breakfast. Nibbling along Derek's bottom lip, he trailed his kisses over the stubble-covered chin to his neck.

Derek's head dropped to the side, giving him more skin to play with. He scraped his teeth over the man's jugular and Derek jerked.

"Max, soon," Derek warned.

"Come on, baby," Max growled and squeezed.

"Ah," Derek grunted as heat spilled over Max's hand onto his stomach.

As the hot liquid washed over his flesh, Max let his control go and came, adding his to the mess. Derek collapsed on him, trapping their hands and dicks between their bodies.

Wincing, Max wiggled and shimmied until their hands were free. He threaded the fingers of his clean hand through Derek's hair and stared up into the blue sky. The strangest feeling of contentment swelled in him and he imagined that this was the most relaxed he'd been in a long time. Since he'd left Sydney for America, he'd been searching for elusive happiness and though he knew the relationship he had with Derek wasn't going to end well, he would grab what he could before the singer had to go back to the real world.

"Am I expected to move any time soon?" Derek mumbled into Max's shoulder.

Max chuckled. "You're not, but I am. I need to help the hands round up some of the bulls. We're shipping them to a rodeo in Cheyenne."

He heaved a mental sigh as Derek rolled off him and flopped to the ground beside him.

"A rodeo, huh?" Derek sounded intrigued. "I've never been to one."

"You're a country singer and you've never been to a rodeo?"

He pushed to his feet and staggered over to the creek. Shivering, he stuck his hand in and washed it. With a silent curse, he cleaned off. Damn, the water was cold. He tucked himself back in and fastened his jeans before he turned to see Derek watching him. After strolling over to snatch his shirt off the ground, Max slipped it on and winked at his lover while snapping it up.

"I freely admit that I grew up in the city, spending my weekends and summers in Virginia horse country. There aren't many rodeos there, but tons of horse shows."

Max eyed Derek's tight ass as the man climbed to his feet and copied Max's actions, washing and dressing. He turned to search out his hat before Derek could catch him staring. He tugged it on and waited for Derek to join him.

"Why'd you pick country music to sing if you're not a country boy?" He gestured at the horses.

Derek had no problem slipping Betsy's bit back into her mouth and they were ready to ride in minutes. Swinging up into the saddle, Max grinned at the almost natural way Derek rode the mare. By the time Derek left, he would be riding like he was born to it.

"I liked the way most country songs told stories and I wrote my own stuff. Maybe I'm a country boy at heart." Derek shrugged. "I don't know. It's what I fell into, I guess."

"I'm not complaining." Max glanced over to where a group of hands were riding towards the bulls' pen. "Would you like to come and watch us? You'll have to stay out of the way though."

"I can do that."

They cantered over to join the rest of the men. The hands were polite to Derek, but they didn't act any different with him than they would with any other cowboys. Their quiet acceptance was one of the things Max found most interesting about the men who worked with him. Whatever their opinion on him being gay, they kept it to themselves. What seemed to matter most with these men was how he did his job, and as long as he continued to do it up to their standards, they wouldn't cause him any trouble. As long as Derek didn't act like he looked down on them because they worked with their hands, they would take him on his actions. So far, Derek hadn't done anything to upset them and Max didn't see that happening any time soon.

Chapter Nine

Derek hummed softly as he checked his reflection in the bathroom mirror. The tune had floated in his head since that afternoon when he had watched Max and his men gather the bulls that were shipping out tomorrow for the rodeo. It wasn't complete and he didn't have any lyrics, but they would come in time. He'd learnt early on in his song-writing career not to force anything. Forcing was the quickest way to lose the flow.

"Are you ready?"

Turning, he saw Max lounging in the doorway, thumbs hooked in his jeans and hands framing the tempting bulge Derek was quickly getting addicted to. He strolled over, rolling his hips as seductively as he could. Max's eyes lit up with lust and the man's breathing sped up.

Reaching out, he cupped Max's jean-covered erection and squeezed hard enough to make Max grunt.

"I'm more than ready."

Max grasped his wrist and pulled his hand away, shaking his head at Derek. "That's not an option at the moment."

He pouted. "Your bosses won't be mad if you're a little late. They might even understand."

"They'll understand far too well." Max tugged on Derek's arm, leading him down the hall and stairs.

Derek drew up short as a thought hit him. "They aren't upset about us, are they? I don't want them to fire you because of this. I'll tell them it was all my idea. I seduced you."

A strong yank and he smacked against Max's chest. Embracing him with muscular arms, Max leant down, kissing Derek with a firm touch. Derek slid his hands up over Max's shoulders, burying his fingers in the curls at the nape of Max's neck. He opened, letting Max take what he wanted, giving the other man all he could at the moment.

Only when air became a precious commodity did they ease apart. Derek rested his forehead against Max's and sighed, enjoying the music of his lover breathing. A quick slap to his ass broke the moment and he stepped back, rubbing the stinging cheek and frowning at Max.

"The seduction was mutual and they're only worried you'll break my heart when you leave."

Max walked out of the door and Derek had no answer to his statement. Derek feared the breaking would go both ways. His heart wasn't getting out this relationship without a few scars.

He caught up with Max as he stepped onto the front porch of the main house. Laughter could be heard from inside and Derek hesitated at the threshold. How long had it been since he'd hung out with people who weren't interested in what he could do for them? He doubted that any of the men would have a demo CD for him to listen to or a friend who wrote 'crazy good' songs.

"Are you coming? They won't bite." Max paused. "Well, they won't bite you. They might bite each other and I don't want to think about that."

They went in and after Max hung his hat up, they wandered into the living room. Brody and Tony were there, chatting with another couple. Derek recognised Leslie Hardin and the younger, dark-haired man at Les' side had to be Randy Hersch, Les' partner.

"Here they are." Tony gestured for them to come closer. "We were debating whether we should send out a search party for you two or just eat without you."

Derek grinned as Max blushed when Tony leered at them. Tony's teasing made Max uncomfortable, so Derek shifted all their attention to him. Holding out his hand, he approached Les.

"It's great to see you again, Mr Hardin. I wanted to thank you for suggesting I come out to Brody's ranch for a vacation."

Les smiled and the crow's feet at the corners of his brown eyes crinkled. Derek remembered thinking how gorgeous those eyes were when he was younger, but he didn't remember seeing the level of happiness in them that was evident now.

"Please call me Les. I'm glad to be able to help. When Edward called me to ask for help, I knew our place wasn't quite what you needed." Les grinned at Randy standing next to him. "At times, our house seems to be equipped with a revolving door. People are always coming and going. Tony's place is quieter most of the time, and I figured that's what you needed."

"You were right. This place is exactly what I needed to relax." He flashed a bright smile at Randy. "I'm Derek St Martin."

"Trust me, I know who you are." Randy shook his hand with a firm grip.

"Yes, he does. We have every CD you've made and he's probably memorised all your songs." Les rolled his eyes, but his teasing held a loving tone.

"Stop or we'll have to talk about your unnatural addiction to Irish drinking songs."

"You promised we wouldn't discuss that in public." Les pouted dramatically.

They all laughed and Derek relaxed. These men were good friends and seemed more than willing to open their circle to include him. It would be weird, even if the friendships only lasted while he was there, to have male friends. He'd isolated himself from all the men he knew except Eddie, because of the potential for scandal. While these four men were honest about their own preferences, they would never force him to 'out' himself if he didn't want to.

"Do the other riders know you're gay?" He blushed as they all looked at him. "Sorry. I didn't mean to blurt that out, or even ask that actually, but I was wondering."

Tony shrugged and handed his empty glass to Brody to refill. "Some do, but I don't advertise it. More guys would probably be fine with it than I think, yet why rock the boat if I don't have to?"

"Good philosophy." Derek nodded his thanks as Les handed him a beer.

"I've got another five good years on tour before I start getting too old to ride. As long as my body holds up and I don't get injured, I should be okay. And if Brody's willing to stick with me through it, I'll wait until I'm done riding before I announce to the entire world I like guys."

He looked at Brody. "Doesn't it bother you?"

"What? Having to refrain from grabbing his tight ass behind the bucking chutes or biting my lip to keep from kissing him whenever he has a great ride?" Brody smiled, encircled Tony's waist with his arm and drew the bull rider to him. "Sure, it bothers me, but I love him and I'm willing to do it for as long as he wants. Love is about compromise, isn't it?"

Derek thought about that as the others talked. His parents had never compromised about anything. They'd gone their own ways and that was probably why they'd ended up getting a divorce. By the time his mother had married Eddie's father, Derek had given up hope of any of her marriages working.

He watched how Brody, Tony, Les and Randy acted around each other. There was no way one could see them and not know they were couples. Les seemed to always know where Randy was in the room. Brody made sure Tony always had a drink. It was like watching two couples doing intricate dance numbers, conscious of their partner every moment.

Max eased up behind him, resting his hand on Derek's hip and whispering in his ear. "It's interesting to watch them together. You can tell who belongs with whom, but the four of them are connected as well."

He nodded, but was more interested in the warmth emanating from the man behind him. Shifting, he leant back, letting Max support his weight, and bit back a groan as Max's erection rubbed against his ass.

"Have you talked to Edward lately, Derek?" Les turned back to him with a smile.

Stiffening, he started to move, but Max tightened his grip on him and wouldn't allow him to step away.

Why was he worried? It wasn't like these men hadn't stood in that same position before. He returned to resting against Max and shook his head.

"No. Eddie's competing up in New York, plus he was going to hang out with his dad for a week or so. I try not to bother him while he's riding or dealing with his father."

"Fathers can be a pain in the ass," Randy muttered.

"Yeah. Eddie has to be the parent and not because his dad's getting senile or anything. Sometimes having too much money spoils people. Mr Monterrose is very demanding, which is probably why my mother left him. She wants everyone's attention to be on her. At times, it was like being with two five-year-olds, always demanding your complete adoration."

"Do you see your parents much?" Brody perched on the arm of the chair Tony sat in.

Les and Randy took the couch and snuggled close, leaving the smaller love seat for Max and Derek. They sat and, without thinking, Derek rested his hand on Max's thigh.

"My dad died in a freak scuba diving accident off the coast of Australia when I was ten. My mom emails me once a year or so from wherever she happens to have landed at that moment." Derek frowned. Had he heard from his mother lately? He'd have to check.

"I'm sorry to hear that. I always believed everyone should have one member of their family they liked," Les commented.

Max laid his arm along the back of the loveseat and Derek settled into a space that seemed made just for him. He grinned at Les.

"Don't be sorry. I have Eddie and that's the only family I need. We talk as often as we can and get together whenever we have time. Mostly we've been able to meet up in different cities while I was on tour."

"Sounds like a good relationship." Randy glanced at Max. "How about you, Max? You have any family you like?"

"No."

Max's abrupt denial startled everyone for a minute and Derek remembered that Max's mother was dead. Obviously, he didn't want to talk about his father.

"Okay, Les, I have to ask. How the hell did you get into rough stock breeding? I mean it's obvious why Tony's breeding bucking bulls, but why would a blue-blood Virginian chose to raise mean horses and vicious bulls?"

Again Derek took their attention off Max, understanding that while his lover didn't have a problem with these men and probably liked them, he wasn't willing to share his life story with them either.

Not being an idiot, Les accepted Derek's change of topic without argument. "The bulls were something I sort of fell into. I wasn't interested in breeding show horses anymore, so I thought I'd try my hand at something else. The bucking horses? Those were more to help out a friend of Randy's."

"The better you get to know Les, Derek, the more you'll come to realise that Les likes to pick up strays, which is why we're now breeding cutting horses, bucking bulls and broncs for the rodeo. He owns a small women's boutique in San Diego, so my brother's fiancée has a job out there."

Randy's tone was teasing, but his love for Les shone through.

"So if I ever need help with my singing career, I can come to you?"

"Sure, I think I can afford to support a dead-beat country singer." Les winked at them.

Tony pushed to his feet. "Come on, gentlemen. Time to start the grill and get some steaks cooked."

They all filed into the kitchen to help with supper.

* * * *

"I think I drank too much," Derek slurred as Max slipped an arm around his waist to help him up the steps onto Max's back porch.

"Hanging out with those guys can do that to you," he commented, remembering the last time he'd spent the night, playing cards and talking with Brody and Tony.

"Les tends to stay away from alcohol because of the medicine he still takes for his head, but Randy can give Tony a run for his money at times."

Max grinned at the serious expression on Derek's face as his lover tried to make his feet work, lifting them higher than normal.

"I thought you were a professional drinker," he teased as he got the door open without losing hold of Derek.

"I drank whisky and it doesn't do anything to me except make me pass out. Beer, on the other hand, makes me silly."

"And makes you regret all the drinking the next day?"

Derek nodded his head and groaned. Not bothering to turn any lights on, Max led the way up to his room where he stripped Derek down to his boxer briefs before getting him set up in the bathroom.

"Brush your teeth and get ready for bed," he ordered, propping the man up at the counter before handing him his toothbrush and toothpaste.

He headed back downstairs to lock up, confident that Derek would be able to complete those two tasks without help. After checking the windows and doors, he went back upstairs. He heard Derek yell his name as he got to the top.

"Max!"

Jogging to the bathroom, he froze in the doorway and his jaw dropped. Derek sat on the toilet, toothbrush in hand. There was toothpaste everywhere, but on the brush. Somehow, Derek even had it in his hair.

Derek pouted, his bottom lip trembling. "I can't get the toothpaste on my brush."

Biting his lip to keep from laughing, he took the offending items from his lover's hand and managed to get the right amount of paste on the brush. He handed it back to Derek.

"Do you need me to help you stand?"

Derek glared at him, weaving slightly as he pushed to his feet. "I'm perfectly capable of brushing my own teeth."

"Of course you are."

Okay, maybe letting Derek drink hadn't been a good idea, but Max didn't think the man would relapse into his normal drinking patterns. There were other ways for him to tire himself out now and Max could keep an eye on him, since they were living together for now.

Derek listed to one side, but managed to get his teeth brushed without further incident. Max cleaned up the mess and got them both into bed. They snuggled together and he smiled as Derek's soft snores filled the air. All in all, it had been the most fun he'd had with his bosses in a long time, though he admitted he'd never made much effort before this to spend time with them.

Chapter Ten

Adrenaline raced through Derek at the cheering of the crowd at the rodeo in Cheyenne. He squirmed in his seat, knowing they weren't voicing pleasure for him, but still his body reacted like he was on stage.

"You all right?" Max leaned over and whispered.

He nodded and contained a shudder as another roar ripped through the people around him. A saddle bronc and rider burst from the chute, bucking across the arena. Dust and the cowboy flew as the rider lost his seat. The bronc charged away, not wanting anything to do with the man he'd successfully thrown.

"What do you think so far?"

"I like it. It's different from performing, but has the same feel to it." He let his hand brush Max's thigh quickly before reaching up to adjust his hat.

Max had offered him a cowboy hat before they left the ranch to travel down with the bulls, but Derek had refused. He knew it would be too easy for someone to recognise him, since he wore a hat when he was on stage. The ball cap he'd got from Tony along with his sunglasses seemed to be doing the trick.

"You want to walk around? I need to check on the bulls."

"Sure."

Derek sprang to his feet and climbed down the bleachers with Max. He clenched his hands to keep from grabbing Max's tight ass as he walked in front of him towards the holding pens behind the chutes. The rodeo wasn't the best place for him to forget himself. Too many people and too many chances to get his ass kicked.

Averting his eyes, he glanced around, enjoying the anonymity he experienced. He could be himself and not pretend to be 'Derek St Martin'.

"Hey, Max, you bring some of Tony's bulls down?"

Derek studied the stocky blond bull rider greeting Max. The man moved stiffly and didn't seem able to bend well.

"Cody." Max grinned. "Tony said you might be here. You aren't riding yet, are you?"

Max rested his hand on Cody's shoulder instead of giving him the back-thumping greeting Derek had seen him give other cowboys. What made Cody different?

Cody gave a slight shake of his head. "No. The doctors say I have another six months of therapy before they'll even consider letting me ride. Of course, since this is my second back injury, they aren't keen on me competing at all."

"Can't say I blame them, mate," Max said. "Another injury and you could be wheelchair-bound."

The bull rider's eyes dimmed. "What am I supposed to do? I'm not ready to settle down and be a farmer like my dad."

Derek heard the desperation in Cody's voice. It truly did sound like riding was in Cody's blood.

"I know, but be careful. We don't want you to be killed next time."

Shifting, Derek brought Cody's gaze onto him. A quick head-to-toe glance and Derek had to wonder about the whole gay cowboy thing. Shit, they seemed to be coming out of the woodwork since he'd got to Tony's ranch.

"This is my friend, Derek. Derek, this is Cody Harwood. He was Tony's travelling partner until Tony settled down."

"Nice to meet you."

They shook hands and Cody studied him intensely, but whether the man figured out who Derek really was or not, Derek didn't know.

"Yeah. Once Tony fell for Brody, he liked to go home between events instead of driving to them every week. Can't say I blame him all that much. If I had someone like Brody waiting at home for me, I wouldn't want to spend a lot of time away from him."

Cody's voice was low and couldn't be heard above the crowd—he probably didn't want anyone to overhear what he was saying.

Someone called Cody's name.

"You want to grab a bite to eat and a drink afterward?" Cody asked as he turned to walk over to another group of cowboys.

Max glanced over at Derek and he nodded. "Sure. We'll meet you behind the chutes after the bull riding."

"Catch ya later, then."

"He seems like a nice guy," Derek commented as they made their way to where the bulls they'd trucked down were corralled.

"He is. Two years ago, he got in a bad wreck, broke his back and it took him about seven months to get back to riding. Early in the season this year, he wrecked again and injured his back. Different place and he can walk, thank God, but he's rolling the dice each time he climbs back on one of these beasts." Max waved a hand at the bulls.

Derek studied the animals in front of him. Each bull weighed in at around a ton of muscle. Max had explained these bulls were just as much athletes as the riders. They were fed special diets and were treated like prize show animals. He'd choked when Max told him a great bucking bull could be sold for a half a million dollars, though he shouldn't have been surprised. The show horses Eddie competed on could bring that much or more when they were sold.

Max leaned over the fence and rubbed the nose of a large black bull. "When you see RM Monarch here out in the pasture, you'd never think he's one of the rankest bulls on tour. He likes to have his butt scratched and will follow you around, begging for carrots. But put him in a chute and when he bucks out, he's trying to throw the rider off, and then once he does, he'll go after him. I've seen him step all over a man while hooking one of the bullfighters. Yet once he's back home, he's as nice as can be."

Was Max pulling his leg? No way would he treat that walking steak like a pet. Those horns looked like they'd skewer a man without much effort. If it stepped on him, it would probably break his foot.

"I'll take your word for that." He laughed.

"Let's grab a hot dog and get back to our seats."

After meandering over to the food booths, they got hot dogs and sodas before heading back to their seats. They settled down in time for the bull riding to start. Derek winced and cheered with everyone else as the men pitted their strength against that of the bulls. He held his breath as one cowboy went down and the bull nailed him in the back with a hoof. There were a few tense moments, but he shouted along with the crowd when the rider stood and waved to them.

"Of course, he probably has a couple of broken ribs," Max murmured to him.

Keeping an eye on the rider and the two men helping him out of the arena, Derek saw him collapse as they shut the gate behind him. He turned back to meet Max's gaze.

"They have an image to maintain. Tough guys like that don't let a little thing like a bull kicking their ass get them down."

Derek understood what it was like. "Just like the music business. You can't let anyone know if you're unhappy or strung out. You always have to present a good strong face to the public."

"Doesn't sound like much fun."

Derek's laugh was harsh and he shook his head. "Why do you think I'm here instead of back in Nashville?"

"You only needed some extra-curricular activities to tire you out."

Max winked and Derek blushed. Why was it different when Max flirted with him? On tour, both men and women flirted with him, letting him know in very unsubtle ways they would be willing to share his bed, if he wanted them. He never did. Too scared to cross that line, despite the women he'd slept with. Yet when Max smiled at him, Derek had to keep from throwing caution to the wind and kissing the man like he was starving and Max was the only piece of food in the area.

Were part of his urges simply the fact that while they were at the ranch, they didn't have to refrain from touching each other? Had he got used to being able to show his attraction to Max? Or was there something specific about this cowboy, drawing him like a moth to a flickering candle?

His want must have shone on his face because Max's dark eyes heated and the man licked his lips, like he was looking for a lingering taste of Derek's own mouth on his.

"Have you seen enough?"

Derek couldn't talk, his mouth and throat were dry, but he could nod.

"I'll let Tip know we're heading back to the hotel." Max stood and handed him the keys. "Meet you at the truck."

He watched Max climb down the bleachers and make his way through the crowd to the bull pens. It was only when Max disappeared behind the chutes that Derek stood and managed not to shove people out of the way as he hurried to the parking lot.

Leaning against the truck, he watched couples wander past and couldn't help smiling at the young teenagers who stopped every few feet to kiss like they needed each other so much. They were in their own little world, not caring what people thought of them, and he envied them that security.

One young lady glanced at him as she walked past, flashing him a bright smile. Derek nodded back at her and she stopped, head cocked to one side, studying him. He tensed, sure she was going to recognise him.

"Didn't I see you with Max Furlo?"

He kept the bill of his cap pulled low. "Yes, ma'am."

"He's a good man. I wondered if Tony was going to send him with the bulls this year. Tell him Martha said hi."

"I will."

She winked and leaned closer, whispering, "I loved your concert in Nashville last year at the CMA Music Festival."

"I don't know what you're talking about," he stuttered, not really prepared for someone to guess who he was.

"Don't worry. I won't spill the beans. A man's got his right to privacy, same as the next."

Tugging on the bill of his cap, he smiled. "Thanks, ma'am."

She gave a little wave and continued on her way. He rested his head back against the cab of the truck and stared up at the sky. The stars twinkling in the dark velvet matched the odd bubbling of happiness in his chest. Who knew he'd have to go to cowboy country to find the tranquillity he needed?

A hand slapped his shoulder and he jerked upright. Max grinned at him.

"You ready to go?"

"Yes. What about Cody?"

"I told him we were going to clean up and to call when he gets back to the hotel. He's staying at the same one we are. We'll hook up there."

They slid into the truck and Derek let his hand rest on Max's thigh, heaving a silent sigh at finally being able to touch his lover.

"I think getting you in a nice hot shower would really make me look forward to tonight."

Max started the vehicle and drove sedately towards the hotel, managing to keep them on the road, since Derek couldn't keep his hands to himself. He slipped his hand between Max's legs and squeezed gently. Max jerked slightly and glared at him.

"I'm trying to drive here."

He chuckled. "I'm not stopping you from doing that, baby."

"If you're not careful, you're going to make me drive off the road and how do I explain that to the police officers?"

"You could probably come up with something." He dragged his palm over Max's erection, rubbing it hard for a second before sitting back.

"You are an evil man, Mr St Martin."

"Not evil, just spoilt. I'm not used to having to wait for what I want."

Max turned into the parking lot and stopped the truck. "Get out and upstairs. I'm going to park. You better be naked when I get to the room."

Derek jumped from the vehicle and strolled with purpose through the lobby to the elevators. He clenched his hands to keep from pushing the button insistently. God, he should have taken the stairs.

* * * *

Max double-checked the truck, not wanting to forget to lock it because his brain had headed south and all he could think about was the naked man stretched across his bed. His cell phone rang as he jogged across the lot towards the hotel.

"Furlo," he barked as he pushed into the lobby.

"Hey, Max, checking in on you." Tony's voice came over the phone.

"Things are going great here. Bulls are performing the way we like and giving the riders high scores if they make it." He pushed through the growing crowd, murmuring his apologies to people he ran into.

"Good. Is Derek enjoying his first rodeo?"

Shit, it sounded like his boss was settling in for a nice long chat. He didn't want to get caught on the phone, not when he had the sexiest singer in the country spread-eagle in his bed. Derek better be naked and ready for him when he got up there.

"Seems to be having a good time." He slammed his hand against the call button for the elevator.

"Am I calling at a bad time?" A smile tainted Tony's question.

"Well, I am on my way up to the room at the moment."

That was all he was going to say to his boss. Tony could figure the rest out on his own.

"Oh really? And where is Derek?"

"In the room," he ground out.

A warm chuckle washed over him. "Ah, I see why you seem a little short with me. I'll let you go. Call me tomorrow after the rodeo's over. I want to know how the bulls do."

"Will do, boss."

"Have a good night, Furlo. Don't do anything I wouldn't."

"That leaves a wide range of things I can do."

"Bastard." Tony hung up.

Max tucked his phone back in his pocket as the elevator arrived. He made it inside and pushed his floor's button. Slumping against the back wall of the car, he stared down at his feet, not willing to make eye contact and pleasant conversation with anyone he might know sharing the elevator with him.

He practically ran down the hallway once he was off the car. Cursing under his breath, he fumbled with the key card and the door lock. He bit back a shout of triumph when he got the door open. Max barrelled through it then froze, barely avoiding the door as it swung shut.

"Fuck," he breathed, almost swallowing his tongue at the sight greeting him.

Derek was naked, kneeling on the bed with his fingers buried deep in his ass. The singer moaned as he rocked back and forth. Each push back took his fingers farther in and Max watched, thinking that it was the most beautiful thing he'd ever seen.

He must have made a sound because Derek glanced over his shoulder and flashed him a wicked grin.

"Why aren't you naked yet?"

Derek's demand broke the spell Max was under and he struggled to strip off his clothes. A sharp tearing sound ricocheted through the room as he jerked his shirt over his head, but Max didn't care if he'd ripped it or not. All he could think of was getting inside that firm ass and making Derek scream his name.

"Max, I need you," Derek whimpered.

Glancing around, he tried to remember where they had thrown the lube and extra condoms from their morning activities. Damn, where were they?

"Here. They're right here."

Derek nodded over to his left side where the bottle of lube and a foil package rested on the wrinkled comforter.

"You've been busy, sweetheart."

He crawled onto the mattress and settled on his knees behind Derek. He reached out and ran a hand over Derek's tight ass before slapping it lightly. Derek twitched, but didn't stop fucking himself. Max slid his hand around Derek's hip to encircle the man's dripping cock. A tight squeeze and a quick pump had the singer calling his name.

Max grinned, leant forward, and placed a soft kiss at the base of Derek's spine. "Someone got started without me."

"You told me to be ready for you," Derek panted, his free hand wrapped around the headboard.

"And now that it's something you want, you're good at following orders," he teased.

He snagged the foil package without taking his other hand off Derek's dick. He tore it open with his teeth and managed to roll it on without letting go of anything. Tapping his lover's hip, he positioned himself at Derek's hole.

Placing his hands on the headboard, Derek arched his back and Max moaned at the sight of Derek's ass offered up to him like that. He pushed in, drawing a low cry from Derek. Once he was buried as deep as he could, he stilled, allowing his lover to get used to him again.

Max leant forward and brushed a kiss over the nape of Derek's neck and the man shuddered as Max's hard-on slid a little deeper.

"Oh."

Derek shifting slightly was the sign Max had been waiting for. He gripped Derek's hips tight enough to leave bruises and started riding, pulling out a little farther each time and slamming back in harder. He wanted Derek to feel it when they were at dinner later that night.

Max nudged Derek's legs wider. It changed the angle and Derek gave a strangled scream as Max nailed his gland.

"Right there." Max chuckled.

Soon enough, words were as far beyond either of them. Skin slapping skin and the bed springs squeaking were the only sounds filling the room.

Before his brain fuzzed out, Max had the thought that the people in the rooms next to them had to know what they were doing. When Derek tightened his channel around Max's cock, Max decided it wasn't important enough to worry about.

He prised his hand away from Derek's body and reached around, fisting Derek's shaft and pumping in rhythm with their fucking.

"Harder. More." Derek begged and Max gave it to him.

They lost their graceful movements and collided with every stroke, each one forcing the other closer and closer to the abyss. There was no fighting the need or pleasure dragging them under.

Derek tensed, threw back his head, and shouted. Hot liquid covered Max's hand and the blanket under them. He rode Derek through his climax, letting the tremors running through his lover to take him over the edge. His cum filled the latex surrounding his length and he wished they could have done it without any barriers between them.

Yet he knew that Derek was leaving soon and there had never been talk of anything more between them except for the sex. Max shook his head. There was no point in worrying about any of that stuff. Taking each day as a separate moment in time was the best way to survive their fling without too much heartbreak.

As Derek slowly collapsed onto the bed, Max got his hand out of the way and they both sighed as his soft cock slid from Derek's ass. He rolled off and went to clean up in the bathroom. Carrying a washcloth, he came back to wipe Derek off. He tossed the damp cloth back in the general direction of the bathroom, making a mental note to pick up it before they left for dinner.

Max crawled under the covers and held up the edge for Derek to slip next to him. They snuggled close, with Derek's head resting on Max's chest. He glanced at the clock.

"We probably won't have time for a nap. The rodeo's over for the night, so Cody should be calling any minute now."

"Ah, but we can still bask in the afterglow for a few minutes before we have to get up. Do you want to take a shower?"

"We can be mature about it and shower together. It'll be faster."

Derek laughed. "Are you sure? I don't think I have enough willpower to keep my hands to myself with you standing there all wet and glistening."

He snorted. "You're a charmer, but it won't work. We clean up, go enjoy dinner with Cody, and when we get back, you can have your way with me."

"I like the sound of that," Derek purred, nuzzling Max's jaw.

Max pinched Derek's ass. "You would, you horndog."

His cell phone rang before Derek could retaliate. Max dived for his jeans hanging off the corner of the cabinet holding the TV. Derek howled with laughter as Max landed on his ass, still managing to snag his jeans. He yanked his phone out and answered it.

"Furlo."

"Hey, man, you ready for dinner?" Cody's voice was almost drowned out by the background noise of country music and people talking.

"We can be in about ten minutes. You want to meet us down in the lobby?" He struggled to his feet, untangling the bed sheets from around his ankles.

"Will do. See you in ten." Cody hung up.

Max flipped his phone closed then tossed it on the chair next to him. Turning, he glared at his lover, who still chuckled softly.

"You think that was funny?"

"Oh God, yes." Derek winked at him.

"What if I hurt the tender part of my anatomy enough I wouldn't feel up to being taken advantage of later on?" He huffed and headed towards the bathroom.

Derek shot to his feet and followed him, crowding him into the shower stall after he turned the water on. He gasped as Derek fondled his ass with firm fingers. The singer crushed their mouths together and Max slid his arms around Derek's shoulders. The fury of the kiss eased and they nibbled gently, devouring each other's mouths with soft urgency. Max was discovering he enjoyed those quiet moments of kissing and touching almost as much, if not more, than he did their lovemaking.

He eased away. "We can't go much further, baby, or I'll be nailing you against the shower wall."

Derek's smile was pure sex and lust. "See, you don't need to worry about your ass hurting. I'd rather you fucked me anyway."

Reaching for the soap, he shook his head. "Who knew you'd be such a pushy bottom?"

"I never said I didn't want to fuck you, but what can I say?" Derek scrubbed his soap-covered hands over his chest. "I spend so much time being the tough Alpha male, sometimes it's nice to let someone else be in charge."

Max eyed him sceptically. "If I believed you weren't completely in control of any situation you're in, you could sell me a bridge or two."

His lover stayed silent and they rinsed off quickly. Drying and dressing took a little longer. They got down to the lobby in fifteen, instead of ten minutes. Cody leaned against a pillar, texting someone on his phone.

"You hungry?" Max didn't put his full strength behind the slap to Cody's shoulder. He could tell by the brackets around the younger man's mouth that the bull rider was in pain.

"Yeah. I have to eat something before I can take my painkillers. If I don't, I get sick to my stomach."

Derek trailed behind them as they entered the hotel's restaurant. Max noticed his lover talking softly to their waiter before joining them. They ordered drinks and food. Once they were alone, Cody studied the two of them.

"Are you guys together?"

His question was low, but Max glanced around to make sure no one was sitting too close. If anyone figured out who Derek was, he didn't want any of them to remember hearing that particular question.

Derek took a swig of his beer and nodded. "Came to Wyoming for a short vacation. Needed to rest and unwind from my last tour. Max has been taking care of me."

"I bet he is." Cody winked at Max with a purely wicked grin.

Max blushed and ducked his head. God, he hated being made to feel like a teenager with his first crush. He needed to man up and deal with the teasing. None of his friends meant anything by it. They were simply happy to see him spending time with someone, even if that someone happened to be one of the most famous people in the country.

"You let him be, Cody. Unless he's teased you about your love life." Derek stepped in to ease Max's embarrassment.

"Well, now that you mention it," Cody drawled.

Max shook his head. "I never once said anything to you about anyone you might be seeing."

"That's because I doubt you ever noticed them."

"You have a point there." Max chuckled.

Cody turned his gaze on Derek. "I'm not sure if Max notices any of the guys who come and go at Tony's ranch. He's much too focused on his work."

"It took a special type of cowboy to catch Max's attention."

"Yeah, one who can sing, not ride," Max commented.

Seeming to be unable to not tease Max himself, Derek leaned in and whispered, "You didn't mind how I rode you earlier tonight."

Max flushed beet red and Cody howled with laughter.

"Oh man, you've got to tell me what you said to him. I've never seen Max turn that red in my life."

Shooting him a nasty glare, Max growled, "I'll get you for that."

"I'm planning on that."

Their joking set the tone for the rest of the night. After dinner, they went to one of the local bars where the rodeo people hung out. Joking and roughhousing with the riders made Max remember why he enjoyed going to the rodeos. He ensured Derek had fun, but hoped no one had a phone to capture a picture of the singer sneaking a kiss in a dark corner with him.

Derek didn't seem worried about being discovered and Max decided to let it go. For one night, he wanted to think about his lover being an ordinary man, not some superstar. They behaved themselves enough to survive the night without getting their asses kicked by a bunch of drunk cowboys.

Later that night as they cuddled under the blankets at the hotel, Max stared up at the ceiling. Watching Derek interact with everyone at the bar gave him insight into the man. Derek loved people and being in the middle of a crowd, though being able to be who he really was, and not pretend, made the man glow even more. He wasn't 'Derek St Martin'. He'd been just plain Derek tonight and Max could see how the last bit of tension had eased out of his body. He vowed to ensure Derek always felt that way while he was with Max.

Chapter Eleven

"Derek, would you do me a big favour?"

He looked up from where he sat on Max's porch. Brody stood at the bottom of the steps. Gesturing to the rocking chair next to him, he nodded.

"If I can, I'll be glad to help."

Brody sat down and nudged Derek's notebook with his foot. "Getting some work done?"

Derek set his guitar aside and leant back in his chair. "I've written more in the last two and a half months than I have in the last three years."

He spread his arms wide to encompass the amazing view of the Rocky Mountains in the distance.

"With so much inspiration, how could I not write?"

"I grant you there isn't a prettier place on God's earth than Wyoming, but I think it's more than the scenery." Brody grinned.

"More than the scenery?" Derek nodded towards two younger ranch hands wandering through the area between the houses. "Are you sure? Because not just the natural world is providing great scenery now."

Brody threw back his head and burst out laughing. "You're a dog, you know that?"

"Of course, I am, but I only look and comment. I don't touch."

"Really?" Brody raised an eyebrow and tipped his head in the direction of Max, who had stepped from one of the barns to talk to the hands.

"All right. I usually don't touch." He shrugged. "Call me weak or crazy. I don't care. This is a moment out of time for me. I can be whoever I want without someone judging me for it."

"What happens when you have to go back to Nashville?"

What would happen? He'd go back to hiding behind a façade and pieces of his soul would start dying again. He didn't want to discuss it, not even with himself, because after a while, it began to sound like he was whining about his life. All things considered, his life was pretty good. He'd signed his first contract eight years ago, knowing the score about having to keep his orientation a secret.

Okay, he might not have grasped the full ramifications of it, but he'd wanted to be a star badly enough to lie to himself about how easy it would be.

"What kind of favour did you need?"

Brody accepted the change in subject. "I know you're here in hiding, but I wondered if you'd be willing to sing a song or two at Yancey's birthday party next week."

"Really? How old is he going to be?" Derek rocked back and forth, staring at Max across the yard, but not really seeing his lover.

"Twenty-one."

He chuckled. "That's an important age."

Frowning, Brody studied the floor under his feet. "It might be, if Yancey hadn't already experienced more in his twenty-one years than most men ever do their entire lives."

Derek chose not to pursue the story he heard in the hoarseness of Brody's voice. The man was becoming more than just a former employee to him, he was becoming a friend and Derek didn't want to jeopardise it by prying too deeply.

"I can do a few songs. Will this make your little brother the most popular man on campus?"

He picked up his stuff before standing. It was time to start dinner — Max would be coming in soon.

"Probably, if he cared about that kind of shit, but he's only concerned with his studies and Juan." Brody stood and shook his head. "Those kids have been crazy about each other since they met."

Derek caught Brody's gaze and winked. "Must run in the family."

Chuckling, Brody punched him lightly on the arm. "You could be right, man."

After waving goodbye to Brody, he went inside and set his guitar and notebook in the corner of the living room. He headed into the kitchen to get the steaks ready for the grill. Humming a melody he'd been working on, he got the potatoes wrapped in foil and a salad cut up.

He wandered out onto the patio and lit the grill. The bright blue of the sky caught his attention. It was Max's shout through the door that brought him back to earth.

"Derek, I'm going up to take a shower."

"Okay. I'll throw the potatoes on now and wait until you're back down here to cook the steak," he yelled back.

"Fine with me. Can you grab me a beer?"

Max disappeared up the stairs as Derek stepped back inside. The shower kicked on, bringing a smile to his face. Just that morning he and Max had spent a pleasurable forty minutes playing in the water before his lover had to go to work. His cock stiffened, causing him to think about joining Max upstairs, but he shook his head. Max had worked hard all day and deserved a good meal, after which Derek would help him relax.

His cell phone rang as he pulled two beers out of the refrigerator. There was only one person he'd talk to while on vacation, so he checked the caller ID. Answering the phone, he tucked it between his chin and shoulder while he opened the bottles.

"Hey, Eddie, how's things?"

His stepbrother laughed. "Good as can be expected. How are you doing?"

He paused for a moment, thinking about Eddie's question. Setting their drinks on the table, he wandered over to the railing of the deck. He stared up at the mountains in the distance.

"I'm doing great, better than I thought I would be when I headed out here." Resting his elbows on the rail, he smiled. "Lots of nice scenery, bro."

"Have you taken advantage of any of the local eye candy?"

"Eye candy? You know I don't go for girls." He frowned.

"No, idiot. I meant the cowboys. I was out there last year to work with Les for a week. I saw some of the men wandering around the ranch. I figured you'd enjoy at least looking at them." Eddie sounded like he'd checked some of those cowboys out himself.

"I didn't think you swung my way."

"Hey, if you're attracted to a person, it really doesn't matter what parts they have." A verbal shrug was evident in Eddie's voice.

"Learn something new every day. Why didn't I notice that before?" He scrubbed his face with one hand.

Eddie sighed. "You were busy, man. Other things on your mind and it wasn't like I was confused or anything. It's sex, pure and simple. Doesn't matter who I'm having it with. It's not like I'm settling down any time soon."

That was true. Eddie had got wanderlust from his parents, along with an inability to form any lasting connection with people. Well, most people. He and Eddie had connected the day they met and they worked hard to stay in touch.

Still, guilt welled in him. Another example of how self-centred he'd become over the years. As his career had taken off, he'd become so caught up in the lifestyle and hiding who he really was he'd lost track of the important things. Thank God, Eddie always reached out to him, even when he'd forgotten birthdays or holidays.

He snorted softly. What a selfish prick. "I haven't been the best brother, have I?"

"Come on, Derek. Don't beat yourself up about not knowing I like guys and girls. I could have mentioned it at some point, just never thought it was important. I guess I could get mad at you for never coming out and telling me you liked guys."

"But..." Derek stopped and thought on that.

Eddie had never asked him about his preferences. He'd always pointed out attractive men to Derek while they were hanging out alone, but he'd never said he knew Derek was gay. Why had he never commented on Eddie's acceptance before?

"How did you know?"

"I walked in on you and one of your boyfriends while you were still living at home. You didn't notice. Probably because his face was buried in your groin." Eddie snickered.

"And you didn't say anything afterward?" He turned when he heard footsteps come out onto the deck.

Max glanced at him on his way to the grill where the steaks waited to cook.

'Eddie', he mouthed and Max nodded.

"It was embarrassing and completely hot, besides being uncomfortable. I mean you were my brother." Eddie exhaled sharply. "I was trying to figure out what I wanted, men or women. It hadn't occurred to me then that I could have both if I wanted. If I confronted you about being gay, then we would have ended up talking about me and I wasn't ready for that."

"Understandable." He tipped his head back and closed his eyes. "When I get back to Nashville, we'll spend some time together. Maybe re-connect without the drugs and alcohol in the way."

"Sounds great."

Silence reigned between them for a minute or two.

"Derek, you sound happy, man, for the first time in a long time. Whatever—or whoever—you're doing out there agrees with you."

Laughing, he nodded, even though Eddie couldn't see him. "I'll admit that one piece of scenery is keeping me busier than usual."

Max shot him a confused frown while Eddie's mirth echoed over the phone.

"I'm glad to hear that. I'll try and call you in a couple of weeks. I have some shows to compete in, so I'll be on the road for a while."

"Ride safe, Eddie. I'll talk to you soon."

After hanging up, he stared at his phone until Max strolled over to him and kissed his cheek.

"Things okay with Edward?"

Nodding, he turned sideways, resting his hip against the railing and letting his hand brush over Max's hip. "Yeah. I was thinking about what a bastard I am."

Max took the phone from Derek and tossed it on the side table next to the grill. He slipped his arm around Derek's waist, allowing the singer to rest on him. Nuzzling Derek's dark curls, he breathed deeply.

"If Monterrose told you that, I'm not going to let you talk to him anymore."

Derek shook his head. "No, he didn't do anything but tell me the truth. I realised I don't know my brother as well as I used to and it's my fault. Once I became a big star, I couldn't be bothered with things that didn't directly concern me."

The steaks sizzled behind them, but Max wasn't worried about them. His attention focused on making his lover feel better.

Rocking back and forth, he murmured, "You were building your career, love, and Edward had his horses. You simply grew apart."

"But I don't want that. For years, ever since my mother married his father, Eddie and I were the only family we had. Our parents didn't want to be reminded that they weren't getting any younger. Unfortunately, I just figured out I can be just as selfish as they were."

He rubbed his hand over Derek's back. "Hush. I bet Edward said he understood."

Derek nodded.

"Then you can start anew now. You've been made aware of what you did wrong and you can correct the mistake. Make more of an effort to be in your brother's life."

Max bit his tongue, wanting to ask Derek to make room for him in his life. Not fair, he admitted to himself. Something told Max that he meant a great deal to Derek, but at the end of his forced vacation, Derek would leave and Max had no place in Nashville with him.

No more wallowing in self-pity. He'd deal with the fallout when the man left. Until then, he'd enjoy every moment they had together. Sliding his hands down to cup Derek's ass, he grinned. Derek met his gaze with a smile of his own.

They came together, arms wrapped tight around each other. Max kissed Derek, using all the talent in his mouth and tongue to make Derek hum. He loved hearing the man sing while they touched and stroked. Derek didn't even realise he did it, but Max knew he'd be hearing that smooth voice in his dreams when he lay alone in his bed at night.

Max broke their connection only when the scent of burning meat drifted over to fill his nose. Resting his forehead against Derek's, he waited until his breathing returned to normal before moving towards the grill. He peeled the charred pieces of steak off and tossed them on the plate. Derek joined him and they stared down at the ruined meal.

"Well, we do have some pasta and sauce left over from last night," Derek suggested.

"Sounds good to me." Well-done steak was a crime against humanity as far as he was concerned.

"Do you want to check the potatoes while I go heat up the rest?" Derek headed inside, scooping up his phone as he went by.

"Sure. Don't answer any more phone calls tonight," Max ordered.

He smirked at the finger Derek flipped at him. Maybe Derek would leave it inside while they ate. The only good thing was that so far, only Edward had called and bothered Derek.

Max yanked one of the foil-wrapped potatoes off the grill and, after revealing it, he poked it with a fork, making sure it was cooked. It looked good. He took the other one off as well and picked up his beer for a drink while waiting for Derek to return, sitting at the table.

Having family seemed to complicate life as far as Max could see. He'd loved his mother and grandparents, but while they were alive he'd got frustrated with them. He lifted his bottle to the sky, toasting his family. As much as they'd annoyed him, he would take that over being alone any day.

"Eddie didn't call to roust out bad memories, Max. He was just checking to see how I was doing." Derek slid one plate in front of him. He took the seat across from Max and grabbed one of the potatoes.

"I know." He added butter and a little salt to his own vegetable. "Do you mind telling me what he said that made you decide you were a terrible brother?"

Derek swirled some spaghetti around his fork and took a bite. While he chewed, he must have decided what to tell Max. After swallowing, he set the fork down and glanced over at him.

"Usually, I wouldn't share confidences, though I don't think he'd care if you knew."

He reached across the table and laid his hand over Derek's. "You don't have to tell me anything if it makes you uncomfortable."

"Not uncomfortable. Just stupid. How could I have missed this rather important piece of my brother's personality?"

Max eased back, letting Derek take his time in telling him.

"Eddie's bisexual."

Max eyed Derek, trying to remember what Edward Monterrose looked like. He'd met the man at some point while he was at Hardin's ranch. Not very tall, but well-built for his size. White-blond hair and bright blue eyes that watched everything with intense interest. Or maybe he had been checking out the ranch hands.

"I'll admit he doesn't give off strong 'interested in guys' vibe." He shrugged. "Of course, I didn't really pay that much attention to him. He was another client of Hardin's and didn't have anything to do with me."

"Maybe he tilts towards women more than men. I didn't ask him, but when I get back to Nashville, I'm going to try and rebuild what I let go the last couple of years."

"Good idea," he agreed.

"What about you? Do you have any siblings to worry about or annoy you?"

Tension tried to sneak into Max's muscles. Talking about Derek's family was one thing. Discussing his was something entirely different. Yet sharing was what people did when they were in a relationship and what he hoped to have with Derek beyond a summer fling.

"It was just my mum and grandparents. No brothers or sisters." Max pushed his plate away.

Derek seemed to sense Max didn't want to talk about it, but didn't seem willing to let him off the hook. "No father in the picture, huh?"

He stood, stalking over to the edge of the deck and propped his hip on the railing. "He was only around to get Mum pregnant, then he moved on to better things."

"Did you know who he was?"

Max started when Derek slipped his arms around his waist and pulled him back against Derek's chest.

"Not really." That wasn't a lie.

"At least you had your mother and grandparents. Eddie and I just had each other."

Derek's warm breath washed over his ear and Max shivered, his cock going hard. He pushed his hips back, moaning as the length of Derek's erection rubbed against the seam of his jeans.

His lover slid one hand down to cup Max's dick through his clothes, massaging in rhythm of thrusts against his ass. He dropped his head back onto Derek's shoulder, breathing faster.

"Maybe we should clean up out here and take this inside," Derek murmured, then nipped his ear and another shiver raced down Max's spine.

"Okay."

They picked everything up as fast as they could and made their way upstairs where they proceeded to enjoy the rest of the night in each other's arms.

Chapter Twelve

The voices slowly died down as Derek walked out on the makeshift stage. He sat on the stool, hooked the heel of his boot on the rung under him, and smiled at everyone gathered around him. He propped his guitar on his thigh.

"Oh my God, that's Derek St Martin."

Surprised whispers flew through the afternoon air and he saw a few guys elbow Yancey with grins on their faces. Yep, the young man was definitely going to be big man on the campus when they got back to Cheyenne after the weekend. Yancey shook his head and gestured for Derek to continue.

"You all know who I am. I happened to be in the area and thought I'd drop in to wish Yancey a happy birthday. I think you'll recognise this song."

He started playing his biggest hit, closing his eyes and listening to the audience singing along with him. God, Derek missed the days when he'd played small clubs and intimate settings. Oh, he loved the huge arenas and sell-out crowds. The energy those kind of gigs created had helped him through a few shows during a long tour, but there was something special about the smaller venues.

Opening his eyes, he searched the crowd, looking for one specific face. Max stood at the far edge of the crowd, leaning against the fence with an intense expression on his face. He slipped into the next song, keeping the tempo fast and upbeat. People danced around him and he found himself wishing he could get Max out on the dance floor. He bet his lover would be a great dancer, considering how he moved when they made love.

"This next song is one I wrote a couple days ago. You get to be my guinea pigs. I hope you like it."

The first haunting notes drifted over the hushed anticipating crowd. Max straightened from the fence and Derek knew the man recognised the music.

"I walk alone
Searching for a place
Wishing for a home
Safe and strong.
Winds beat me.
Suns burn me.
I'm looking for shelter
Cool and quiet.
With one touch,
You soothe me.
I see
The deep honest truth.
No matter the places
Our lives take us
You are
Where home lies."

He never took his eyes off Max while he sang, hoping his lover understood who the song was about. They'd never talked about what would happen when he had to leave, but he couldn't keep his feelings secret. At least, not in his songs.

As the song trailed off, silence reigned for a few seconds before everyone started clapping. He stood and handed his guitar to Randy, who carried it inside before Derek moved off the stage and wound his way through the crowd. He stopped to sign autographs and get pictures taken. There weren't a ton of people, so it didn't take him long to get to the spot where Max had been standing. Glancing around, he searched for Max.

"He headed out to the yearling barn," Yancey murmured as he passed by.

"Thanks."

The younger MacCafferty nodded and gathered his friends to him, not allowing any of them to follow Derek. Entering the dimly lit barn, he looked around.

"Max," he called softly, not wanting to bother the yearlings.

"Down here." Max stepped from one of the stalls farther down the aisle.

When he got close enough, Max reached out and fisted the front of Derek's shirt. His arms flailed as Max yanked him into the stall and pinned him against the wall. Before he could say anything, Max crashed his lips into Derek's. His gasp allowed Max entrance and his lover plunged his tongue in and stroked over his teeth. Derek shivered, shoving his hands through Max's hair and knocking his hat off.

Max grasped his ass and ground their groins together. He let his head fall back and bounced off the wall as he groaned.

"Shit, Max."

A low growl rumbled in Max's chest as the cowboy rocked them together. Derek dropped his hands between them, fumbling with belts, buttons, and zippers. He fished out his cock and Max's, pumping them quick and hard. Max braced one hand on the wall next to Derek's head while joining Derek's hand with his other.

Derek rested his forehead against Max's and they stared down as they pleasured each other. He gripped Max's shoulder, knowing he was probably going to leave bruises, but he didn't care. Their breathing synced into harsh pants and their hips established a rhythm that drove them closer to the edge.

"Derek," Max pleaded.

"Yes."

Speeding up, he tightened his grip and dragged Max's hand over their erections, shoving hard to push Max over the edge.

"Fuck." Max groaned as he stiffened and wet heat spread over their entwined fingers.

The smell of Max's cum and the shudders racking his lover's body drove Derek headlong into his own climax. His spunk joined Max's and he closed his eyes as the pleasure rushed through him.

Max collapsed against him, trapping their hands between them. Derek leaned his head back, resting it on the wall behind him and trying to calm his breathing.

"What got into you?" He managed to roll his head to meet Max's gaze.

"Your singing. I've heard you sing before, but tonight it felt like you were singing just to me."

Derek raised his clean hand and traced the line of Max's cheek. "Maybe because I was."

Max's eyebrows shot up. "And that last song?"

"It's how you make me feel," he admitted in a low voice.

"Damn."

He frowned as Max pushed away and walked out of the stall. Derek stayed where he was, trying to figure out what had just happened. Did Max feel the same way? Or had their relationship only been a summer fling? Derek confessed to himself that was how it had started for him, but as the weeks went by, he'd grown closer to Max than anyone else, except for Eddie.

"Here."

Looking up, he spied Max standing in the stall door, holding out a cloth. He took it and cleaned up best he could. Max took it back when he'd finished, and leading the way out of the barn, he tossed it towards a bucket in the tack room. Derek yanked Max to a halt before they left the barn.

"Are you mad at me about something?"

Max shook his head and shoved a hand through his hair. "No. It's just I didn't expect this." He waved a hand between Derek and him.

"Expect what? That I might come to care for you?"

"Yeah." He cupped Derek's face. "Give me a little time, Derek. I'm not mad. I simply need to wrap my mind around it."

He nodded, accepting Max's request. "Okay. Just don't shut me out."

Max kissed him hard before stepping back and adjusting the hat he'd picked up from the floor of the stall. "Let's go and mingle for a little bit, then maybe we can sneak away without anyone noticing."

"Sounds good to me."

They headed back to the main house, not touching, but close enough to brush against each other while walking.

Chapter Thirteen

Derek's phone rang while he and Max cuddled on the couch, watching one of Max's westerns. Snatching it off the coffee table, he glanced at the ID and frowned.

"Who is it?" Max rubbed his hand over Derek's shoulder.

"My manager."

Dread filled his stomach. He knew what Thomas wanted, but for the first time in his career, Derek wasn't looking forward to go back into the studio. He didn't want to leave and go on tour, visiting twenty-eight cities in twenty days or whatever fucked-up schedule his record company planned for him.

He wanted to stay at the ranch, to wake up every morning wrapped in Max's arms and drift to sleep with the music of Max's breathing in his ear.

"Go ahead and answer it. It might be important."

Max paused the movie and pushed to his feet. The look on his face told Derek his lover didn't believe the words he spoke. As Derek flipped open his phone, Max walked out of the room.

"Hello, Thomas."

"St Martin, how are you doing, man?"

Cringing at the jovial tone in Thomas' voice, Derek dropped his feet to the floor and rested his elbows on his knees. "Pretty good."

"Ready to get out of there?"

He stood and wandered over to the window. Opening the curtain slightly, he looked out to see Max stride across the yard, heading towards the foaling barn.

"Not really. I actually like it here."

"Seriously?" The surprise in that question made Derek smile.

As he eyed his lover's ass covered in faded jeans, Derek replied, "Yes, seriously. No rat race around here."

"Glad to hear it, but you're needed back here in Nashville, Derek. Time for you and the band to head back into the studio. You have one more album to do to fulfil your contract with the record company."

He sighed and turned, pacing in front of the fireplace. "I know and I've written quite a few songs. Great place for inspiration."

"Hey, that's great. We can bill it as all-new Derek St Martin songs. Your fans will eat it up."

Somehow, he couldn't find the excitement. He stopped and stared at the one framed picture on the mantel. It was of him and Max at Yancey's birthday party. Someone had captured the photo when they'd returned from the yearling barn before rejoining the party. They stood with their arms around each other, foreheads touching, lost to the world around them. He remembered thinking that moment had to be the most perfect one he'd ever had in his entire life.

Derek had the feeling he would be looking back on the past three months and deciding they were far more important than any tour he ever did, but still, he was a professional and he had obligations. As much as he didn't want to leave, he had a life to get back to and a career he did enjoy for the most part.

"I think they're some of my best stuff." He shot a look over to where his guitar and notebook rested against the wall in the corner of the room. Max never complained when he got up and started composing a new song. The man really did seem to understand the artist's compulsion to create.

"I'm sending a car to pick you up at five tomorrow morning. I already have a jet chartered to fly you back to Nashville and we'll get you into the studio the day after."

He could hear the prison bars clanging shut behind him as Thomas planned out his every move. No more. One thing he'd figured out while in Wyoming was that he was in control of his life. It was his career and it was time to grab a hold and head down whatever path he chose. He wasn't ready to give up singing yet, but he could put his foot down and make some decisions. He wouldn't be lead about like a child.

"I'll go back into the studio next week. I still have a few songs to finish up and I would like to rest a little before we start recording."

"You can't take too long. Three months should have been enough to rest up," Thomas protested.

"Thomas, I'm not arguing with you. I'll fly back to Nashville tomorrow like you want, but I won't go into the studio until next week or when I feel the songs are right."

He hung up on his manager and tossed the phone on the couch before heading out to look for his lover.

Derek found Max by the fence, watching the foals play in the paddock. Joining him, he rested his shoulder on the top rail, studying Max's sad face.

"I have to head back to Nashville," Derek informed him.

Max nodded. "I know."

"The band's getting restless and it's time for me to record my next album. They weren't happy about giving me the three months the doctor ordered."

Max stayed silent.

"You could come with me. Maybe take some time off and I can show you around my town." Derek bit his lip.

"I don't think so."

"I'm going to pack. A car's coming to pick me up in the morning." He traced the lines of Max's face with his gaze, memorising his chiselled chin and high cheekbones.

Derek headed back to Max's house, blinking back tears. He wasn't going to beg.

"Derek, things okay?" Yancey asked as Derek ran into him in the yard.

"Yeah. I'm heading back to Nashville tomorrow, so I have to pack." He summoned up a smile for the younger man.

"If you need anything, let me know." Yancey didn't try to stop him.

Making it to their room, he sat down on the bed and took a deep breath. He brushed tears off his cheeks. Okay, he was an adult. He'd look at those three months as a summer fling. Something he'd never done before, so maybe he'd made it into something more important than it was.

Max had become someone who knew him and understood everything about him. He touched the shirt Max had given him. After folding it, he put it in his suitcase.

He decided to take a shower before grabbing something to eat. He didn't feel like joining the others for dinner. After heading to the bathroom, he turned the water on.

* * * *

"What did you say to him?"

Max didn't turn to look at Yancey. He had nothing to say to the young man. At the moment, he wanted to be left alone to nurse his broken heart.

"Nothing." He glared at the horses in front of him.

"That's why he was crying when I ran into him inside." Yancey climbed up and sat on the top rail.

"Crying?" Max's chest tightened. He didn't want Derek to regret anything that had happened between them.

"You know those artistic types, emotional about everything. He had to know it was a silly little fling." Yancey's voice was casual.

"I know what you're trying to do, kid, and it's not working."

"If you do, then why are you letting him pack thinking this didn't mean anything to you?" Yancey poked him in the arm.

"He asked me to go with him," he admitted.

"And you said no, I bet," Yancey grumbled. "Why?"

Max bowed his head. "I have my reasons."

"I don't care. All I know is Derek risked everything to have a relationship with you. He's in there, his heart broken and you're standing out here being all tough and macho." Yancey jumped off the fence and pushed Max. "Derek St Martin fucking loves you and you're going to fucking throw it away."

Max swung around, hands clenched. "Don't push me, Yancey."

"You're nothing but a coward, Max, living on this ranch and never having to deal with real people. You're letting the best thing in your life leave tomorrow." Yancey glared at him, anger flushing his cheeks.

"That's enough, Yancey." Brody stepped between them. "Dinner's ready."

"But he's…" Yancey protested.

"I know. Now go inside," Brody ordered.

Yancey refused to leave, but Brody stared him down. Max didn't care about the power struggle between the brothers. He knew Yancey had a point. He needed to explain to Derek why he'd turned him down.

"Sorry, Max," Brody apologised after Yancey stomped away. "I think he's still hurting because Juan chose to stay out East instead of coming home for his birthday."

Max shrugged. "He's right. I have to talk to Derek, but I'm not sure how. I've never told anyone."

"You love him, don't you?" Brody touched his elbow.

"Yes." There was no reason to deny the truth. He loved Derek with his entire soul, but he knew even love couldn't survive their worlds.

"Tell him. I've seen love outlast some harsh times. It just might surprise you."

Nodding, Max made his way back to his house. After climbing upstairs, he knocked on the closed bedroom door.

"I really don't want to talk about it, Yancey." Derek's red eyes and tear-stained face registered shock when he saw Max standing in the hallway.

"May I come in?" He was worried that Derek would shut the door in his face.

"You made it pretty clear outside you didn't have anything to say to me. Why now?"

Derek's hurt-filled words told Max he had wounded him. It was the one thing he'd never wanted to do.

"I do have something to say. So much that it's crowding my mind and tangling my tongue." He reached out to touch Derek's cheek, but let his hand drop when Derek stepped away from him.

"I'm not gifted with words," he continued. "It's hard for me to say what I feel or want. I'm much better with action."

Derek moved back into the room, leaving the door open. Max took it as a sign he was willing to listen to him. He followed, noticing the damp auburn curls at the nape of Derek's neck and how the white T-shirt he wore moulded to his lean chest. His cock twitched and he swore silently. Now wasn't the time for his libido to kick in.

Derek sat on the edge of the bed, giving Max the option of sitting next to him or standing. Max chose to stand. If he joined Derek on the bed, he'd never say what he needed to say. He wanted Derek desperately, with a primal urge to imprint the singer's scent in his mind.

Max stared at Derek until he squirmed.

"What did you have to say?" Derek demanded.

"My heart wants to tie you up and hide you away. It's telling me not to let you go," Max confessed.

"You don't have to let me go. Come to Nashville with me." Derek's eyes sparkled.

"No, I can't. If I went with you, we'd come to resent each other." Max shook his head. "No matter how much we loved each other, we wouldn't be happy."

"Why not? We'd be together all the time except when I was on the road and even then you could come with me." Derek got up and walked over to Max. Putting his hand on Max's arm, he stroked him.

"That's just it. We would be together as friends except for some hurried moments when we eked out enough alone time. You could never introduce me as your lover." Max covered Derek's hand and gripped it. "I refuse to be hidden like someone's dirty secret. I saw first-hand what a relationship like that can do to both partners."

"Do you love me, Max?"

Derek's question was simple, but Max's answer was far more complicated than yes.

"More than anything or anyone in my life, but you can love someone that much and still resent the hell out of him." Max sighed, dropped Derek's hand and paced the room. "I told you that my mother died nine years ago."

"Yes." Derek moved back to the bed.

"When you asked about my father, I said I didn't know him." Max stopped in front of the window again, staring out into the deepening night. "It was true, but not in the way you took it to mean."

Derek sighed. "I'm not in the mood for riddles, Max. Just tell me."

"I knew my father's name. I'd see him as he'd pull up in front of our house, but usually I was in my grandparents' car, being driven to their house for the weekend."

He closed his eyes, reliving the overwhelming need he'd felt as a child for his father to see and acknowledge him. It had never happened and by the time he'd been a teenager, he'd no longer cared.

"It was a classic romance story. Two teenagers meet and fall in love. Mum was from the poorer side of town, but she was beautiful. Father came from an upper-class family. Old money, and his mother would have had a heart attack if she ever found out about Father's girlfriend." Max's laugh was harsh. "So they agreed to keep their relationship a secret."

"What about when you came along? How could they keep you a secret?" Derek moved to the middle of the bed, sitting cross-legged and resting his elbows on his knees.

"Not sure, except they involved my mum's parents. To most of the town we lived in, I appeared one day and was explained away as an orphaned nephew, though I don't think anyone was fooled for long." Max paced towards the hallway.

His nerves sparked. For so many years, he'd kept his family experiences private, shoved deep in the back of his mind. No one needed to know about his messed-up life. It wasn't like his was the only dysfunctional family out there.

"Mum got a job in Sydney and we moved there. Of course, my father helped pay for everything. That's what any reasonably loving man would do for his mistress."

"Mistress?"

Max swung around and smirked. "Yeah. No fairy tale ending here. My father ended up marrying some society girl his parents liked. He stayed married to her for twenty years, all the while sneaking around and cheating on her with my mum."

"Wow. Twenty years? They must have really loved each other," Derek murmured.

"They did or at least, Mum really loved my father. Maybe he loved her too." Max shrugged. "I don't know. I never spoke a word to him. I never even met him face-to-face. Mum made me promise I wouldn't."

"Why not?"

"It would expose them and hurt his standing in the community."

He stopped by the window. His scowl was reflected by the glass back at him.

"Committing suicide three days after my mum's funeral didn't do much for him either."

"Fuck. That sucks, man."

He saw Derek shift like he wanted to come to him. Max hoped Derek stayed where he was because Max would never finish telling him his burdens.

"Worse yet was the note he left his wife, telling all about his love for my mum and how he'd never loved his wife." He twisted around to look at Derek. "Selfish bastard. He should've lied to her like he had all their lives together. Why did he develop a backbone after Mum died? Why couldn't he have had the strength to marry her in the first place?"

Derek held up his hands in an 'I'm not sure' gesture. "Maybe the secret worked for them." He smiled.

"I know, but you would have to keep me a secret and I won't live ashamed of who I am and who I love." Max folded his arms across his chest and glared at the floor.

"What do you want me to do, Max?" Derek shot to his feet. "Give up my career for you? Say fuck all those years of struggling to make it. Screw all my fans and people who've supported me. Do you want me to throw it all away and come be a cowboy with you?"

Max raised his gaze and met Derek's. "No, I don't. You're not meant to be a cowboy, love. You were born to sing and I'd never ask you to give it up. You'd hate me if I asked and you did."

"You said we'd end up resenting each other if you came back to Nashville with me. Why?" Derek didn't back down.

"I'd come to resent you because we could never openly be together. We'd have to hide from the public and I won't do that. For the first twenty-two years of my life, I did just that until my mum died. I won't go back there." He stepped closer to Derek. "You'd come to resent me because I wouldn't be able to stop asking you to step out of the closet. It would mean the end of a life you were born to live."

He cupped Derek's stubble-roughened cheeks in his hands, studying the face he'd grown to love and he saw tears in Derek's eyes.

"I'm setting you free, Derek. It's time for the songbird to go back to his world. I'm going to be selfish and say I hope you never find someone else to love. It's horrible of me to admit, but I'd like to think you'll be as miserable as I will be each and every night." He brushed his thumb over Derek's plump bottom lip and leaned in close, his breath bathing Derek's mouth. "Does that make me an asshole?"

"No. It makes you an honest person," Derek mumbled as he pressed their lips together.

Derek knew making love with Max once more was a mistake, but he wanted one more memory to keep him warm at night. No matter how much his heart protested, he knew Max was right. They loved each other, but love didn't give either of them the right to make the other miserable.

"If neither of us finds someone to love," he said, pulling a few inches away so he could look into Max's eyes. "Can I come back when I retire? Can I love you then?"

Max nodded and kissed him.

Their lovemaking was slow and gentle. They roamed their hands over chests and backs. Their lips tasted soft skin at the base of the spine and the back of the knee. Their fingers caressed cocks and asses.

No words were spoken. Each 'I love you' and every 'good-bye' was said with sighs and kisses. Their climaxes didn't explode from them. They flowed like the tears they would cry no more.

Afterwards, they held each other tight, savouring the strength in their arms and the warmth of their bodies as they fell asleep, secure in the moment.

Max was gone when Derek woke the next morning. Brody told him Max was out riding fence. He knew his lover and they had said their goodbyes the night before. No point in dragging out the agony.

His suitcase packed and the car ready to go, Derek said goodbye to his friends.

"Thank you for letting me stay here." Derek offered his hand to Tony.

Tony ignored his hand and gave him a hard hug. "You're welcome. I'm sorry things didn't work out."

Derek knew he was talking about Max. "Don't be hard on him. He has his reasons and I have to admit he's right."

He hugged Brody next. "Take care of him. Somehow I think he'll hurt worse than me."

"We will. Remember if you need anything, don't hesitate to call us or Randy and Les. We're always happy to help friends." Brody's understanding smile brightened Derek's sadness a little.

"It's nice to know someone cares."

Derek climbed into the car, settling back with a sigh. It was going to be hard to get his head back to where it needed to be for life in Nashville, but for the first time, he didn't feel so brittle that'd he'd break apart at any minute.

He glanced out of the window as the car drove past the ranch gates. A horse stood on the crest of a nearby hill. The cowboy standing next to it was silhouetted by the rising sun.

Derek raised his hand and Max mimicked the gesture. He stared at the figure until the car turned on to the road and the ranch disappeared from sight.

"Silent goodbyes," he whispered.

Reaching for his backpack, he pulled out his notebook and started writing.

Chapter Fourteen

Six months later

Derek stared at Thomas, clenching his hands to keep from strangling his soon-to-be ex-manager. If there was ever a time when he wished he hadn't stopped drinking, it was this moment.

"You didn't just say what I think you did."

He couldn't believe the man would have the nerve to say something like that to his face.

Thomas whined, "I didn't do anything wrong. Your accountant must have gotten the numbers mixed up."

Did his manager really think Derek wouldn't see what was right in front of him? Peter had explained all the numbers—net, gross, and where little bits of money had been siphoned off at certain points.

"You're kidding, right?"

It was a stupid question. Derek knew it the moment he asked it. The guilt in Thomas' voice told him more than the man's words.

"I'm letting you go, Thomas. I find I no longer require your services."

The pleasure Derek gained from making the break was enormous.

Thomas' shocked expression reminded him of a goldfish, bug-eyed and mouth gaping open.

"What? Why? You can't fire me."

"I can and I will. I had my lawyer look over our contract. It says I can break our partnership if I feel you are no longer representing my best interests and I don't think you are." He pushed the sheaf of papers into Thomas' hand. "Sign those and get them back to my lawyer. Any objections you might have go directly to him."

"You can't do this to me." Thomas glanced around before he leant forward. "I'll tell all the newspapers you're gay."

"Now you're trying to blackmail me?"

Thomas paled, but didn't back down. "Your fans will desert you so fast, and the record company will drop you like you have a social disease."

"What does that even mean?" Derek shook his head. "It doesn't matter, Thomas. I'm headed to the record company's office after this, and telling them I'm retiring. If they ask, I'll tell them. I'm done living a lie, and making money you can steal from me."

He stood and looked down at Thomas.

"You took advantage of me when I was young and willing to do anything to get a record deal. The mistake you made was thinking I wouldn't grow up, and look at my finances. You thought you could hide everything from me as long as you kept me drugged out of my mind. That's bullshit, Thomas. You do realise I could go to the police and get you arrested for dealing prescription drugs, as well as embezzling from me?"

His former manager shook with fear and anger.

"Just sign the stupid papers and get them back to my lawyer. If he doesn't have them in hand by the end of the working day today, he'll be filing a case with the police."

Derek walked out of the restaurant. His phone rang as he handed the parking ticket to the valet for his car.

"Yes?"

"Hey, Derek."

He grinned at the sound of his stepbrother's voice. "Eddie. How are you?"

"I'm good. I'm driving through Nashville on my way down to Florida for the Winter Horse Festival. You want to meet me for dinner?"

"Nashville's a little out of the way, isn't it?"

"Sure, but it might be the only chance I get to see you before you go back on tour. What do you say?"

"Fine with me, but why don't you stop out at the house? You can crash for the night and if you're hauling horses, they can stretch their legs in the paddocks."

The valet pulled up to the kerb and stepped out. Derek gave the kid a tip before making his way around the front of the car to the driver's side.

"Sounds good, and the horses will love it." Eddie sounded tired.

"What time will you be hitting town?"

"About seven."

He climbed into his car and sat, wanting to finish his conversation before he drove.

"I'll try to be back by then. If not, just make yourself at home. I'll have Roberta get some steaks for dinner. The stalls and the paddocks should be clean. My supplier delivered fresh hay a week ago, so we're good there."

"Thanks, Derek. I want to hear all about your vacation."

Derek thought about Max and a bittersweet laugh burst from his lips.

"I have a lot to talk to you about. I'm making some changes and I want your advice."

"I'll help you all I can, Derek." A horn honked. "Oops. Better get off the phone before I get attacked by an angry driver."

"Be careful and I'll see you at seven."

He hung up and tossed his phone onto the passenger seat. Glancing in the rear-view mirror, he pulled out into traffic. A small smile lifted the corners of his lips. The first link to his old life severed. He had an appointment in twenty minutes to cut ties with one more, and then he would see about rebuilding a better life for himself.

Derek was ushered into the office of top music executive Linda Cable. She was a no-nonsense kind of woman and so stunningly beautiful that if Derek liked women, he would have asked her out years ago.

"Rumour has it you dumped Thomas," she said as she waved him to a chair in front of her desk.

"Good news travels fast, I guess. Left him a little bit ago."

"Yeah, he called to let me know you'd gone crazy and not to let you do anything rash until he talked to you."

Her shrewd blue gaze studied him. He didn't say anything, just let her look her fill.

"You're looking good, Derek. Way better than you were when you came off your last tour." She smiled. "A vacation agreed with you."

"It did." He rested his hands on his knees and looked her in the eye. "I'm not signing another contract, Linda. The album I just finished is the last one I owed you."

"That it was, and from what your producer's been saying, it's your best by far." She got that 'let's make a deal' tone in her voice. "If it's money, I'm sure I could talk the label into giving you more than this last deal."

Derek shook his head. "Money's not the issue, Linda. I've got more than enough to retire from the business now and not miss a penny. It's time for me to get my act together. I can't go back to living on a diet of mind-numbing pills. I have to stop lying to myself."

"The drugs and alcohol I understand, but I don't get the lying part."

He took a breath, steeling himself. Could he do it? Could he take the final step out of a closet that had kept him safe all of his life?

Dark brown eyes and a sinfully sexy smile flashed before his eyes and he knew it was time.

"I'm gay, Linda. Have been for as long as I can remember. When I signed my first record deal, Thomas told me no one could find out I liked guys. Said being gay didn't fit the image of a country star." He shoved his hand through his hair. "What did I know? Figured he probably knew the business better than me. It's been eating me alive ever since."

Derek gathered his courage and looked at Linda. She sat, smiling at him. Confused, he smiled back.

"You met someone."

Her statement surprised him.

"Ummm…yes, I did." He really didn't want to talk about Max.

"Figured as much. If you hadn't fallen in love, you'd have never admitted it and drunk yourself to death. Or you would have waited until you retired like a lot of famous people do." Linda laughed. "Did you think I didn't know?"

He nodded.

"I've watched you ogle the asses of my male interns, but at least I never had to worry about a sexual harassment suit against you."

Linda stood and went to the wet bar against the wall in her office. She poured two glasses of whisky, handing one to him as she sat in the chair next to him. Derek set the drink down, determined to stay on the right path this time, and not fall off the wagon.

"In a way, Thomas was looking out for you." She grimaced. "As much as that kills me to admit."

He chuckled. There had been no love lost between his manager and the record executive.

"Just starting out, you wouldn't have gone as far being 'out', but I think you have a better chance at keeping your fan base now."

"It doesn't bother you?" Derek was a little surprised at her acceptance. He figured she'd be shoving him out of the door. Actually, he knew better than that. Whether Linda agreed with his lifestyle or not, she would have been nothing but professional.

Shaking her head, Linda said, "Who you sleep with doesn't affect your talent, Derek. Ultimately, no matter what happens, being in control of your life will be good for you. I have a favour to ask though."

"Sure."

"Don't worry about signing the new deal until after you finish all the publicity and tour for this new album. Let me do some discreet investigating and see how the market would react to your coming out. It might not be that big an issue and the record label won't lose out."

What she asked of him wasn't horribly difficult. "I signed a contract with the label, Linda. I wouldn't renege on that. I'm willing to wait. I want you to know though, if at any time during this tour I get asked about my love life, I'm not going to lie."

Linda met his gaze with a serious expression. "I know and I'm fine with that. I'll give my bosses a heads-up on the situation."

They shook hands.

"Since you're here, why don't we look at the potential album covers? See if there's any you're fond of."

"I'll be glad to."

He followed her out of the office towards the art department. He had some time before Eddie got into town.

* * * *

Pulling into his driveway two hours later, Derek spotted Eddie's truck and horse trailer parked next to the barn. Two horses grazed in the paddocks.

He put his car in the garage and went inside. He decided to change his clothes before he went to find Eddie. Dressed in jeans and a T-shirt, he padded into the kitchen. He looked out of the sliding glass doors and saw Eddie sitting on the balcony overlooking the pond in Derek's backyard. After grabbing a beer and a soda, he went out to join him.

"Here." He handed the beer to Eddie.

His brother took it with a grunt of thanks. Derek rested a hip against the railing, balanced his soda on top of it before digging out a cigarette. He lit it, breathing in the harsh smoke.

"Decided smoking wasn't so bad after all?"

He grinned over at Eddie. "Lesser of all the evils, I guess."

"Thomas know you're smoking again?" Eddie took a swig of beer.

Shrugging, Derek inhaled another lungful. He exhaled and laughed. "It doesn't matter what Thomas knows or doesn't know. I fired him right before you called this afternoon."

Eddie's feet hit the deck and his brother sat up, staring at him in shock.

"Why? I thought you got along with him."

Derek flicked some ashes into the coffee can of sand he'd put out for his cigarettes. He thought about the eight years he'd worked with Thomas. They had been good years, but he'd never felt like Thomas truly understood where he was coming from, and after talking to the man, he realised why.

"I'm going in a different direction and I don't think he'd be able to help me out anymore. Besides, he's been embezzling from me for several years now."

Crushing out the cigarette, he took a drink, waiting for Eddie's next question.

"No fucking way? That slimeball probably drugged you so you wouldn't notice him siphoning the money. He had to have realised you'd figure it out at some point," Eddie growled in anger.

"Yes, and when I did, there was nothing to do but kick his ass to the kerb. I also dropped a few hints to some people I know, and his reputation won't be so sterling after this." Derek wasn't going to let another young singer get screwed over by Thomas again.

"Can't say that I blame you. Thomas seemed more interested in making money for you. He didn't seem all that worried about your drug use."

There wasn't anything Derek could say to dispute that comment—it had been Thomas who had introduced Derek to the mind-numbing joy of pills.

"You know I haven't had to use any to sleep since I went out to Wyoming."

He turned to see Eddie studying him with a thoughtful look on his face.

"We never really talked about what happened out there, Derek. I just know you were so much happier and more your old self. Did you find something to make you happy?"

"You know I did, but it's complicated and I don't want to talk about him at the moment." He shook his head. "It wasn't even that. No stress. I didn't have to hide or be something I wasn't."

He didn't explain further because Eddie knew what he was talking about. Straightening, he gestured towards the kitchen.

"Ready to eat? We can talk more after supper."

"Sounds good to me."

They worked well together, getting the food cooked in comfortable silence. While they ate, their conversation was easy, everyday stuff.

It wasn't until they were sitting on the veranda that the conversation turned serious again.

"What new direction are you taking, Derek? What happened during your vacation?"

Derek rested his head on the back of his chair and stared up at the star-strewn sky. "I fell in love."

"No shit?" Eddie sounded surprised.

"Yeah. I was as shocked when I realised what happened. It was just going to be a fling. A little fun and a lot of sex with a guy I trusted not to out me, but somewhere along the way, I fell in love."

He closed his eyes and thought of Max's brown eyes. He remembered how it felt being held in Max's arms.

"Sounds like the plot of some romance novel," Eddie teased. "Well, with the obvious exception that you're a guy falling in love with another guy."

Snorting, he flipped Eddie the finger. His stepbrother grinned.

"Why didn't you bring the stud home with you, or was Nashville too big-city for him?"

"You'll think I'm crazy, but I believe he loved me too much to come back here with me."

Eddie frowned. "That doesn't make sense, Derek. If he loved you so much, shouldn't he have wanted to be with you all the time?"

"He told me we would come to resent each other because I could never admit he was anything more than a friend. He'd want more and I'd grow to hate him for asking. He'd hate me for making him ask." He bit his lip and swallowed around the lump in his throat.

"Do you really think that would happen?" Eddie's question was soft.

Derek shrugged, leaning forward to rest his elbows on his knees. He looked out over the water of the pond.

"When I left Wyoming, I would have said no. I never would resent loving Max, even if I had to hide the love. Being back here and seeing how things work here, I think he's right."

He glanced at his stepbrother. "I've seen it happen before. Couples in love get ground up in this business and those are the straight ones. I imagine it's doubly tough on the gay ones."

Eddie reached out and squeezed Derek's shoulder. "I'm sorry, man."

"I know."

He shook himself. No point in mourning the loss of his lover. It had been six months since he'd said goodbye to Max, and Derek had worked a lot of things out in his mind.

"I'm glad you decided to stop by. I'm selling the house. Why don't you walk through and let me know if there's anything you want? I'll have it boxed and shipped up to you in Virginia."

"Shit. You're joking, right?" Eddie looked shocked. "This is your dream place, Derek. I remember how excited you were when you signed the closing papers on it."

Standing, Derek went to the rail of the balcony and studied the garden. He'd designed and picked each individual plant for it. For years before he hit it big, he'd dreamt of a place like this.

"I know. I'd finally found a place of my own, instead of moving from house to house like we did when we were young."

His stepbrother grimaced, obviously remembering living with their vagabond parents, jetting from country to country. Eddie had turned to horses for security and Derek had found his foundation in music.

"Aside from falling in love out west, I found what I lost." He paused and smiled. "I found joy in music again. I'd lost that. Too much touring and too many parties. Recording album after album. Drinking myself to sleep. Popping pills to make myself happy and feel good when I hated every minute of it."

Derek thought about the songs he'd written at the ranch. "In the most basic way, I found myself again and I'm not willing to give that up. Unfortunately, I feel myself sliding back into the life I had before Wyoming."

"Where are you moving?"

"I found a great place outside of Austin—a little ranch with cattle and horses. I closed on it two days ago. There's an outbuilding I plan on turning into a recording studio."

"That was fast," Eddie commented.

"Not really. It's been six months since I came back, Eddie. I recorded the last album I owed on my contract. While I recorded, I thought about everything. I decided Thomas wasn't working out and I didn't want to sign another deal with the label. I talked to Linda today. She wants me to wait before cutting all ties." He chuckled. "She's known all along that I'm gay."

"What did you tell her?"

"I'd think about it. But I want to start my own label. Small independent label where only the music matters, not the personal lives of the singers."

Eddie remained quiet for a few minutes and Derek figured his stepbrother was processing everything through that logical brain of his.

"Sounds like a good but risky business. If you're looking for investors, I'm willing to back you, and I bet Hardin would as well."

Derek had thought about money. He was willing to sink all of his savings into the label, but if he could bring others in, it would help with the financial burden.

"Thanks, Eddie." He pulled Eddie to his feet and hugged him tight for a moment.

"Just paying you back. You've invested in several of my horses when I came begging. Email me your business plan and I'll go over it while I'm in Florida.

Also, I'll let Les know you've got a business deal for him. He'll at least look it over."

Derek smiled, but Eddie met his gaze.

"There's another reason why you did all this, isn't there?"

"The first month back in Nashville was bad for me, and I discovered myself slipping into old habits. I stayed away from the pills, but I started drinking again. It wasn't much to begin with. It never is, but soon I found myself drinking to go to sleep, and that can't happen anymore. I went on a binge one night, and woke up three days later without any memory of what I'd done. I missed two days of recording because of it."

Eddie wrapped his arm around Derek's shoulder. "Why didn't you call me?"

"Because I can't expect you to save me. I need to be responsible for myself. Once I sobered up, I went through and threw out all the alcohol in the house, and sat down for a good long look at myself. I needed to return to the whole emotional place I'd been in while I visited Wyoming. It was inside me, and I had to find it again."

Derek moved over to the railing, and stood staring out over his back yard.

"It took me a few days, but I did it. I cleaned up my act, and started making plans to move out of Nashville. I wanted to get as far away from this place, because it's the whole attitude around here. I did some research and figured out Austin has a booming independent music scene. Since I'm not going to do just country music, I decided it was the best place to be without getting caught up in the rest of the bullshit."

They spent the rest of the night discussing the record label and the ranch Derek had bought. Derek relaxed. It helped knowing that Eddie would support him in whatever he wanted to do.

Chapter Fifteen

Three months later

"God, this is awesome," Yancey shouted into Max's ear when the crowd started screaming.

Max wasn't sure how awesome all of this was, but he admitted he wanted to see Derek in person, and make sure his former lover hadn't gone back to his old ways of dealing with going on tour. He'd read all the tabloid stories about Derek firing his manager because the bastard was embezzling from him.

He'd fought the urge to call Derek and check to make sure he was okay, but instead of picking up the phone, he'd gone out riding. Max hated how every spot on the ranch reminded him of Derek and the time they'd spent together.

"It was way cool of Derek to send us these tickets," Randy yelled from the other side of Max.

Max clenched his jaw and nodded. He looked over at Les who stood next to Randy. Les rolled his eyes at Max, and gestured for him to follow.

"We're going to get some beers," Les told Randy and Yancey.

"All right."

The younger men stepped closer together, dancing to the opening band while Les and Max shoved their way through the crowd towards the refreshment stands. Once they cleared the seats on to the concourse, the sound eased up.

"I don't remember the concerts I went to when I was younger being so loud," Les commented as they went to join a line in front of the beer wagon.

"Neither do I, but of course, I didn't go to too many concerts while I was growing up. Didn't have the money." Max shoved his hands in his pockets.

"I was busy riding, and didn't have any time off for fun." Les bumped his shoulder into Max's. "Are you going to go backstage after the concert?"

"I don't think so."

Les shot him a quick glance. "Why not? You haven't seen Derek since he left. Have you even called him?"

"No." Max moved up in line, keeping his gaze ahead.

He understood not contacting Derek at all was stupid, but he couldn't bring himself to talk to Derek. It was too hard on his heart, talking to the man he loved, knowing it could be years before he saw him again.

"I don't understand it." Les looked around, checking to see how close people were. He stepped nearer to Max. "You love him. Why wouldn't you want to see him?"

They arrived at the counter and Max answered. He ordered the beers for them, and Les paid. Afterwards, they wandered back in the direction of the concert. Les stopped Max before they went into the seating area.

"You have to explain this to me, Max. While Randy rode the rodeo circuit, I did all I could to meet up with him, no matter how difficult it was, because I loved him. I needed to be with him."

"I guess you're stronger than me." Max took a sip of his beer. "Listen, I watched my mum take whatever time my father was willing to give her, but it was only an hour here or a couple days there. He didn't love her enough to spend more time with her. I don't want to be in that kind of relationship."

Les shook his head. "It wouldn't be the same. You know he'd spend all of his time with you, if he could. At the moment he can't. Aren't you being rather cruel to Derek, just to protect your heart?"

"You don't understand, and I can't explain it in a way that would make sense to you." He took a deep breath. "If you decide to go back and talk to him, I'll go and wait by the truck. I just can't do it, Les."

The disappointment in Les' eyes shot into Max's chest, and he realised just how much he didn't want to ever see that look again. When had it become so important Les thought well of him?

"I'm sorry," he muttered.

Les shrugged and turned to head inside the arena. They made their way back to the front row seats Derek had reserved for them. Tony and Brody hadn't been able to come, but Yancey wasn't going to miss the biggest concert of the year. He'd begged Max to take him, so Max had made Randy and Les come with them.

Yancey and Randy accepted their beers with smiles. The opening band wrapped up, and anticipation grew with every minute they watched the road crew set up Derek's stage. Yancey and Randy barely stood still, while Les smiled indulgently at his partner. Max kept his gaze on the stage, trying to spot Derek. He might not want to go and talk to him, but he did want to see his lover, even if he couldn't touch him.

* * * *

Derek stood on the edge of the stage, hidden by the large speakers. He stared out into the crowd, hoping Max had got the tickets and come. He'd been so busy with rehearsals and planning his move to Austin, he hadn't checked.

So many times he'd picked up the phone to call Max, just to see how Max was doing, but he'd always put the phone down. Eddie had asked him why he hadn't called Max yet. He'd never been able to explain what was going on in his head.

He planned on going to see Max when he finished his tour, and the recording studio was up and running. Derek wanted Max to come and live with him on his small ranch. Since he planned on living out in the open. No more hiding who he was, and if it lost him some fans, he'd deal with it.

It wasn't like he needed the money. Even with the amount Thomas had embezzled, Derek still had way more than he'd ever need. After the record had been released, and had gone platinum within weeks, Linda had tried to talk him into staying with the label, but he stayed strong.

His decision wasn't about being able to have Max with him. It was about being honest to himself, and not having to hide who he was with lies, and drugs.

"Here he is. Country's biggest star. Derek St Martin."

The announcer gestured towards Derek, who ran out on stage and started into his first song. He kept the energy high through his beginning set of songs, wanting his audience to scream and dance in the aisles.

Derek sang and danced, using the entire stage and working the audience with smiles and waves. He stepped close to the edge of the stage, crouching as people rushed forward.

"Hey, Derek," a familiar voice broke through the wall of sound.

He glanced up, and saw Yancey standing a few feet away from him. Grinning, he nodded, and Yancey gestured with his head to the spot next to him. In an instant, the world narrowed down to Max Furlo, standing quietly in the midst of the chaotic crowd. Derek's heart pounded even faster, and he longed to leap off the stage, and throw himself into Max's arms. He managed to control his reaction for the most part, except he was pretty sure his face lit up with joy.

Hunger burned in Max's gaze, and Derek knew what song he had to sing next. He straightened, but kept singing. Wandering over to his bandleader, he pointed to the song on the list and mouthed, 'next'. The guitarist nodded with a smile.

After wrapping up the last song, he turned to face the audience. His eyes zeroed in on Max, and Derek spoke right to his former lover.

"This is a song off the new album. It probably won't be released as a single, but it's one of my favourites. It's titled Tamed."

Launching into the song, he returned to the edge of the stage, and while he acknowledged other fans, he kept looking back at Max. Those brown eyes shone with love for him, and Derek put all of his heart and love into the words.

"Not a care in the world,

I ran wild and free.
Believed happiness was
Living only for the moment.

"Didn't need a soul mate
Except for a night.
Never wanted more.
Never saw the point.

"You caught my eye,
Standing silent,
In a crowd of people
Screaming my name.

"A scarred hand
Reached.
A soft word
Spoken.

"With a gentle touch,
You tamed me.
With a whispered word,
You chained me."

Silence reigned for several minutes once the music died, then the audience erupted. Screams and shouts filled the arena while flowers and other items fell onto the stage like rain. Derek waved and bowed.

The band segued into another fast number, and Derek felt energised. More than usual, and he knew it was because Max was watching him. During his ten-minute break in the middle of the concert, he grabbed one of his security guards and pointed Max and the others out to Joey. Derek told Joey to bring them to his dressing room as soon as he could after the show. He explained they were close friends, and Derek wanted to talk to them. Joey nodded, and Derek was confident he would do as Derek told him.

The concert rocked, and Derek ended the show with the song he'd sung at Yancey's birthday party. It was the first single off the new album, and it proved Derek's magic was back. It'd gone to number one with a week of its release. Derek bowed then exited the stage.

His security guys hustled him quickly backstage to his dressing room. Sometimes he had a bus he used, but he'd flown to Denver for the concert. Derek stripped his sweat-soaked clothes off, before washing up in the small bathroom attached to the room. He tugged on a pair of sweats, and the 'Sydney' T-shirt he'd stolen from Max.

Derek was drinking his second bottle of water when someone knocked on the door. After checking to make sure it was Joey, he opened the door.

"Get in here before some crazy fan realises this is my room."

Yancey came in first, his wide-eyed gaze speaking of excitement. After him came Randy and Les. Derek greeted them happily, thrilled to see the men he considered family, but the moment Max entered the room, everyone ceased to exist for Derek.

"What the hell are you doing here?"

As much as he wanted to grab Max and entwine his entire body around his ex-lover, Derek couldn't do that. It didn't matter how long they'd been apart, he couldn't forget how lonely he'd felt since then, and why Max would choose to come here now.

Ducking his head, Max shrugged. "I wasn't going to come back here, but then you sang that song, and I had to say thank you."

"Thank you? For what?"

"For writing and singing it for me. I'd told Les that I wanted to forget about us, and find a way to continue on without you." Max snorted. "I should have known I wouldn't have been able to stay away if I saw you."

Derek didn't spare a glance for the others. He focused his entire attention on Max. "I'm glad you came."

His rigid control broke and he walked up to throw himself into Max's embrace. Their lips met in a desperate, passionate kiss. Derek put all his love and need into the kiss, wanting Max to know Derek hadn't forgotten him.

They eased apart when they couldn't breathe any more. Staring at Max, Derek noted the dark circles under Max's eyes and the tired tilt to Max's lips.

"You're not sleeping," he commented.

"It's not the same without you sharing the bed. Too much room." Max shrugged. "How about you?"

Derek nodded. "Pretty much the same, though on this tour, instead of drinking or drugging myself into a stupor, I usually write."

"Sounds like you've gotten things straightened out," Les spoke up, reminding Derek there were other people in the room with them.

Laughing, he grabbed Max's hand and dragged him over to the couch. Les and Randy took the chairs while Yancey sat in the beanbag chair Derek had requested be brought in before he arrived.

"Yes, it seems the best thing Eddie ever could have done for me was send me to Wyoming. Besides meeting Max and the rest of you, I really got my head on straight out here and figured out what was the most important thing." Derek rested against Max's side, forcing Max to wrap his arm around him.

"Aren't you afraid someone might see you and Max together?" Randy asked, waving a hand towards them.

Derek shook his head. "No. I told my record label I'm not hiding any more. If someone asks me, I'll tell them the truth. I'm not going out and telling the media at the moment, but the time will come when I'm ready. Not while it matters at the moment. No one comes in here without my permission."

He didn't want to say anything about opening his own label yet.

"I saw you fired your manager. Won't he tell the tabloids or something? I haven't heard any rumours on the gossip shows either." Yancey frowned.

"I told him to go ahead and tell everyone. I didn't care, and I still don't, but my lawyer might have scared him into keeping his mouth shut. I'm not sure, because we are pursuing charges against him for stealing from me, and I've basically ruined his reputation in the music industry." Derek shrugged. "You'd think he want to make some kind of money, and some of those rags pay big bucks for a scoop."

Max grunted. "He doesn't want to get in trouble for any more than he already is."

"I don't want to talk about Thomas. Tell me how everyone is doing," Derek commanded.

He cuddled closer to Max while the other three men caught him up on their lives. He was happy to hear everyone was doing well, but he really wanted to spend his time talking to Max. Well, actually he wanted to do more than talk. Unfortunately, he had to leave to catch a plane in an hour, so he didn't have the opportunity to do more than hold the man he loved in his arms.

Les stood after about thirty minutes. "We're going to head to our hotel. Max, you have a key to the room, right?"

Max nodded.

"Good. I know Derek has to leave soon, but you should be able to spend some time alone with each other before he does." Les gathered Randy and Yancey with a glance.

Derek hugged them and called for Joey to escort them out. After the door shut behind them, he turned to look at Max.

"I wasn't going to come backstage," Max admitted, his gaze on the floor.

"Why not?" Derek joined him on the couch, but didn't touch him.

"Because it's going to hurt twice as much saying goodbye to you the second time." Max still didn't look at him.

He reached out and took Max's hand in his. It was only when they finally touched again that Max raised his eyes and met Derek's gaze.

"Is that why you never called me?"

Max nodded. "Yes. It's hard enough to see you on TV and hear you on the radio."

Derek didn't laugh, because he understood how Max felt. It was part of the reason why he'd never called Max either. He wouldn't be able to resist telling Max all about his plans, and he found he wanted to have everything taken care of before he brought up Max coming to live with him.

He checked his watch, and swore. "I don't have much time left before Joey comes to get me. I have to fly out to Los Angeles to do a TV show interview, which I hate because they ask the same questions. Just once I'd like them to ask me something that wasn't a talking point."

"Did you mean it? If someone was to ask you about your personal life, you'd be honest." Max eyed him.

"Actually, if they ask me a vague question about my personal life, I'd tell them it was personal, but if they asked me if I was seeing anyone, I hope I am. If they want to know any more than that, I'll share, but to be honest, most of them don't really care one way or the other. They know I'm there to sell CDs, not spread rumours."

Max smiled. "How is the tour going? You're taking care of yourself better?"

Derek accepted Max didn't want to talk about the possibility of their relationship going public. "Yes, I am. Like I said, I'm not medicating myself with pills or alcohol. I work out, or compose music if I can't sleep. I've got enough songs written already for a whole new album."

"I bet your record label's excited to hear that," Max muttered while he nuzzled the hair at Derek's temple.

"Sure, they are."

Or they would be, if they knew about it, and if I hadn't told them I was done after this one, Derek thought.

Silence settled over them, leaving them the time to soak in each other's presence to keep them company when they were alone at night. Yet Derek understood how hard it was going to be for Max, because he didn't know their separation was coming to an end. There were only three months left of Derek's tour before he was free to start living his life the way he wanted.

Knocking sounded on the door, and Joey peered around the edge. "It's time, Mr St Martin."

"Thanks, Joey. I'll be ready in a minute."

"Yes, sir." Joey nodded to Max before stepping back out into the hallway.

After standing, Derek held out his hand to Max, and helped his lover climb to his feet. They embraced tightly, and Derek breathed in the familiar scent of sweat, leather and horses he'd always associated with Max.

"Don't give up on me, Max. I love you," Derek whispered.

"I'll always love you, Derek, and when you're ready to quit, I'll be waiting."

Max kissed him, and Derek threw all his of love into it, hoping Max really meant what he said about waiting for him. He wanted to shout it would only be three more months, but he contented himself with memorising everything he loved about Max.

Max eased away, resting his hands on Derek's hips. "You need to get going. I'll walk you out to the limo, then I'll catch a cab to the hotel."

"All right."

Derek grabbed his carry-on and his hat. Joey would get the rest of his bags and take them to the limo. They walked out of the dressing room, and Joey slipped past them to gather the rest of the stuff. Derek led the way through the backstage area to where the door leading out to the back parking lot was.

The driver opened the door to the backseat, and Derek tossed his hat and bag inside before turning to Max. "I'll be seeing you some time soon," he promised.

"I know."

Max gave him a quick hug, and a slap on the shoulder before he walked off. Derek dived into the back of the limo in order to keep from begging Max to go with him. It wasn't time yet.

He dug out his phone, and dialled it.

"Hello, Derek. Did you just say goodbye to Max?" Les answered.

"Yes. Thanks for leaving when you did." He leaned his head back on the cushions and closed his eyes. "I appreciate being able to spend some time with him."

"Did you spill your secret?"

Derek laughed. "No, but it was close. Did you and Brody get the papers I had couriered over?"

"Our lawyers will be going over them tomorrow, and we'll be getting back to you. I gave them a quick glance before we left the ranch. Everything looks like it's in order."

"So you're both still interested?"

"For my own investment, yes, I am interested. As far as Brody's concerned, I'm pretty sure he's still a go, but we'll know for sure tomorrow, and we'll do a conference call with you on some things."

"Great." Derek sighed. "After the interviews in L.A., I'm taking the jet to Austin late tomorrow. I have a concert there, and I'm meeting with the architect and the owner of the construction company to start renovating one of the outbuildings to a recording studio."

"Have a good flight then, Derek. We'll talk soon."

"Good night, Les. Tell Randy it was nice seeing him tonight."

Derek hung up and stuffed his phone in his carry-on as the limo pulled up in front of the hanger. The record label chartered a jet for him to use when he needed to fly places other than where his concerts were.

He made his way onto the plane and took a seat. Derek loved to fly, and once the jet was in the air, he'd be fast asleep. He dug his phone out again, and sent

Max a text before he turned it off. He needed to rest because he had five interviews starting really early in the morning.

After the jet took off and levelled out at cruising altitude, Derek put his seat back, and closed his eyes. The last thought in his mind was of Max, like it had been since the day they'd said goodbye the first time.

Chapter Sixteen

Four months later

"Max," Romanos called.

Halting on his way to the yearling barn, Max waited for his boss to join him. Romanos lit a cigarette and grinned.

"Got a minute to talk?"

Max frowned, wondering what Romanos wanted. "Sure. It's your dime."

His boss chuckled. "That's true."

They started walking towards the barn. Romanos took a couple of drags before speaking. "How was your vacation?"

Max didn't want to talk about the two days he'd taken off to go to Cheyenne. He was pretty sure Romanos knew where he'd gone, but it wasn't any of his boss's business. Of course, Romanos thought he was crazy for not going with Derek when the man asked a year ago. Max had never been able to explain his reasons why he hadn't gone, and the longer he was separated from Derek, the weaker his excuses became.

"Fine. It was just two days. Had some personal stuff to attend to."

The look Romanos shot Max said he probably knew exactly what that personal stuff was, but he let it go. "Brody and Les need you to take a trip for them."

Now he was really confused. What sort of trip would include both his other boss and Hardin?

"They need some papers hand-delivered to someone down in Austin." Romanos fiddled with his shirt cuff.

"No one else is available for this?"

Romanos wouldn't meet his gaze and Max wondered what his boss wasn't telling him.

"No. It happens to come at time when we all have other places to go." Romanos tossed the butt to the dirt, grinding it out with his heel.

"Can't they mail it?"

"No. They want it hand-delivered. Important papers or something, I guess."

Sighing, Max figured it wasn't his place to question orders from the bosses. "Sure, I'll go."

"Great."

Max swore he saw Romanos smile when the bull rider bent to pick up the burnt filter from the ground.

"Be ready to leave tomorrow morning at ten. Yancey'll drive you to the airport on his way back to school. You're taking Les' jet down there." Romanos slapped his back. "Appreciate you doing this for us, Furlo."

"Welcome."

He entered the barn and led one of the yearlings out to work with. Something was going on. He could tell from the way Romanos acted, but Max wasn't going to waste his energy worrying about it. Tomorrow would be soon enough to find out.

As for going to Austin, it wasn't like he had a personal life to be interrupted. His smile held a hint of irony. It had been over a year since Derek had left, and Max's life had returned to the uneventful, quiet solitude it had been before Derek arrived.

At night now, he'd go back to his house, eat a frozen dinner, and fill the silence with TV shows. The technique worked well until he headed for bed. His empty bed taunted him with all the possibilities that he'd given up when he sent Derek back to Nashville. Waking up in the middle of the night to reach for Derek drove him to spend those hours until dawn sitting at his kitchen table, kicking himself for letting Derek go.

Yet he knew what he'd told Derek was true. Resentment would rear its ugly head eventually and Max would rather be alone than deal with Derek hating him.

The colt snorted softly to get Max's attention and he started brushing the yearling again, pushing thoughts of Derek to the back of his mind where they would stay until the late night hours.

* * * *

Stepping from the car, Max settled his hat back on and looked up at the building in front of him. He would deliver the papers then grab lunch. Romanos had given him the weekend off, telling him to have fun in Austin. The sly grin on his boss's face increased Max's paranoia that something else was going on.

He walked up to the desk and got the attention of the security guard.

"Can I help you?"

Jerking his hat back off, he ran his hand through his hair and sighed. "Yes. I have papers to deliver to someone at Triangle Records."

He gestured to the envelope he'd set on the counter.

"Let me check and make sure they're expecting you, Mr...?" The guard lifted the receiver and gave Max an expectant look.

"Max Furlo."

Shifting, Max fidgeted with his hat brim.

"You can go on up, Mr Furlo. It's floor seven and they're waiting for you."

Nodding his thanks, he snatched up the file and headed for the elevator. Only a few more minutes and this whole ordeal would be over.

The doors slid open and he walked out into a plush office. The young lady at the reception desk smiled at him.

"You must be Mr Furlo."

"Yes, ma'am. Here's the papers my boss wanted you to have."

"Oh, you need to hand-deliver those to the big man himself. I'll take you to the conference room." She stood and pointed down the hall. "Would you like a cup of coffee?"

He gritted his teeth, trying not to demand to know what the hell was going on. "Yes, thank you."

The receptionist flashed him a bright smile and led him to an office. "Here we go. The boss will be a minute or two. He's finishing a phone call."

She shut the door and Max set his hat upside down on one of the chairs. Stuffing his hands in his pockets, he wandered over to the bank of windows overlooking the park in the back of the building.

As it often did when Max had free time to think, his mind went to Derek. He would have liked a chance to explore Austin with him, and maybe go dancing at one of the clubs. He wasn't much of a dancer, but he bet Derek would be sexy as hell, moving to the music.

"Max."

He remained staring out of the window, sure it was his imagination that made him think he heard Derek's voice.

"Max, look at me."

This time a hand gripped his shoulder and turned him around. Derek stood there, gorgeous as ever with a hopeful smile on his face.

"Derek." He clenched his hands, wanting to reach out, but unsure of what would be accepted in this place.

"Thank you, Sally. Hold my calls and lock the door behind you."

Sally nodded, set the coffee tray down and left, shutting the door behind her. Max was aware of all that on the fringes of his mind. Most of his attention was focused on the man in front of him.

"What are you doing here?" He finally managed to make his tongue work.

Derek grinned. "I own it. Well, technically, I'm part-owner. Hardin, MacCafferty and Eddie all put in some capital for me to start the label."

"I knew there was something funny about them sending me down here," he muttered, rubbing his sweaty palms on his jeans.

"I didn't know they'd be sending you. Your bosses and their friends seem to be matchmaking."

Derek moved to the table, pouring the coffee and offering Max a cup. Taking it, Max shivered when their fingers brushed. He stepped back, putting distance between them.

"Why aren't you in Nashville, Derek? Why your own label?" He held the cup like a barrier to shield him from Derek.

Max's body didn't want to talk. It wanted to strip Derek naked and fuck him on the table, but they had to talk before they ended up in bed together.

"I finished recording my last album when I got back to Nashville. All those songs I wrote at the ranch went on it and it turned out to be my biggest CD so far."

Derek sat on the edge of the table, resting back on his hands and giving Max a good view of his body.

He wore faded jeans and boots. His tight, white T-shirt was covered by an unbuttoned dark blue dress shirt. Max's hands itched to touch the warm skin he remembered so well.

"Happy to hear it. Doesn't explain why you're in Austin though." His voice was gruff.

Derek gave him a knowing look. "Six months into recording, the tension started to set in again. I started drinking more and, to my ex-manager's despair, I smoked more. At least I didn't fall back on the pills."

Max saw hints of exhaustion in the lines at the corners of Derek's mouth. Giving in to his own demands, he reached out and laid a hand on Derek's thigh.

"I'm sorry. It sounds rough, but you looked good when I saw you in Denver."

He bit back a moan when Derek's fingers entwined with his. It felt like centuries since he'd touched this man instead of four months.

"It was. At night, I'd sit on my deck, look out over my pond and wonder where all the joy went. Leaving you was the hardest thing I'd ever done, but I was looking forward to the recording sessions. I've always like the creative part of music more than the selling part."

Derek's callused fingers stroked over Max's knuckles, but Derek stared out of the window. Max stayed silent, not wanting to interrupt Derek's thoughts.

"One day, I saw a guy walking down the street and I thought it was you. After I stopped him and embarrassed us both by hugging him, I went home and drank as much whisky as I could without managing to kill myself. When I woke up three days later with no memory of what I did, I realised I needed to do something about my situation. More than that, though, I could feel myself letting go again. I was sliding back into the habits of numbing the pain."

Max growled, tightening his grip on Derek's hand.

"That binge was a wake-up call for me. I would have eventually dealt with losing you. It would have left a hole in my heart, but I would have survived." Derek gave him a soft smile.

He nodded, understanding what Derek meant.

"Losing myself again? That's different. I wouldn't have survived that. Alcohol poisoning or a nervous breakdown, either one was a possibility for me. I didn't want that. There was a part of me still hoping we had a future together. So I got my act together, made some decisions, and by the time we saw each other in Denver, everything was falling into place. I wouldn't be returning to Nashville."

Derek's admission broke Max's control. Setting down his cup, Max threaded his free hand through Derek's auburn hair and pressed their lips together. He swiped his tongue inside Derek's warm mouth, relearning the taste and feel of him. He pulled back, resting his forehead against Derek's.

"I would have waited until it was right for you to come back to me," he murmured.

Derek laid his free hand on Max's chest. "I know, but I decided it wasn't fair to either of us. Why do we have to wait until other people are comfortable with us loving each other?"

"It's the way of the world, babe." He shrugged.

"Well, it needs to change." A stubborn expression crossed Derek's face, quickly replaced with a grin. "I fired my manager and told my record label I wasn't going to sign a new contract with them."

Derek straightened, forcing Max to move. Keeping hold of him, Derek led the way to a leather couch along one wall of the conference room. They sat and Max wrapped his arm around Derek's shoulder, tugging him close. The scent of smoke and musk drifting from Derek made Max's cock stiffen, but he ignored it. There would be time for that later.

"How did they react to that?"

"Some of them weren't happy, but the executive I dealt with understood. I had fulfilled my contractual obligations and was willing to complete the publicity tour they'd arranged for me. I have one more appearance to make at the ACMs and I'm done."

Excitement rose in Max. Was there a chance they could be together? He didn't want to hope too much.

"I sold my house in Nashville and bought a ranch about an hour out of Austin. I decided to start my own record label. It's going to be a label where the artists are here for the music and unashamed of who they are in real life. I'm not going to let any of my artists feel like they need to hide or lie."

Derek's gaze met his and Max saw everything he'd wished for shining in them.

"Are you sure?" he whispered.

Derek sat up, cradled Max's face in his hands and nodded. "I'm positive, Max. I want you to know this. Yes, I'm doing this because I want us to be together…"

Max opened his mouth to protest and Derek placed a finger over his lips.

"But more than that, I'm doing this for myself. I was losing the joy of the music. I'd been unhappy before I met you and in my darkest hours, I considered quitting and walking away. I never did because I was weak and got lured back into the chaos. Only after spending time with you out on the ranch did I find the courage to say enough was enough."

Derek kissed him and Max's brain shut down. Whatever details remained could be figured out later. Right then, he wanted Derek without doubts or questions. He'd accept the gift handed to him.

He yanked Derek over until the man straddled his lap. Their moans mingled as Derek's erection rubbed over Max's. Filling his hands with Derek's firm ass, he rocked them together.

"Skin," Derek muttered against his lips.

"Is the door locked?" he asked, having a rational moment before all the blood in his body pooled in his groin.

"Yes. I told Sally to lock it when she left." Derek sounded distracted.

"Good."

Surging to his feet, Max held Derek until he found his balance. When he was sure Derek wouldn't fall, he stepped back and reached for his own buckle.

"Jeans off. Naked on the couch."

Lust slowly shut down his ability to speak in complete sentences. Derek's blue eyes lit up and he was naked and kneeling on the couch before Max got his boots off.

"Damn."

Derek's curse caused Max to pause.

"What's wrong?" He ran his hand down Derek's tanned back.

"No lube or condoms." Derek's disappointment was obvious.

"Lube's no big deal. Spit works almost as well." Stopping, Max took a deep breath and laid his heart out there. "We don't need condoms, do we? There hasn't been anyone but you."

Derek tensed and Max wondered what he was thinking. He didn't think Derek had turned into a whore after they'd broken up, but he also didn't believe the man had become a nun. There had to be someone else in the year since they'd last been together.

A shudder racked Derek's body and worry raced through Max. He bent forward, pressing a kiss at the small of Derek's back.

"We don't have to fuck, babe. We can suck each other off and head to your place afterward." Max slipped his hand around Derek's body to fist his shaft. Derek wrapped a hand over Max's to keep him from moving.

"I love you. I wasn't interested in anyone else after I left the ranch." Derek took a deep breath and glanced over his shoulder at Max. "We don't need to use protection. I want to feel you inside me without the barrier of rubber, Max. I want your cum to fill my ass."

Gripping Derek's chin, Max gave him a bruising kiss.

"Thank you," he mouthed against Derek's lips.

He let go of Derek's face and gave his length a squeeze. Derek's eyes rolled as he pushed his cock through Max's palm.

"I'll take care of the lube."

Max sucked on his fingers, getting them good and wet. Spreading Derek's cheeks with one hand, he rubbed his slick digits over the puckered hole he'd revealed. He pressed one tip against Derek's opening and breached the ring of muscles.

Derek arched and pushed back, taking Max in. Crouching down, Max bit one ass cheek and Derek yelped. The sting of the bite distracted his lover enough for Max to slide two fingers in.

"God, I've missed this. I've missed you." Derek's soft declaration warmed Max's heart.

"I never forgot the feel of you riding my length or how full I felt when you fucked me," he admitted, stretching and preparing Derek for his dick.

Derek dropped his head forward, accepting Max's invasion and as his body relaxed, Max spat in his palm and slicked up his shaft.

Positioning the flared head of his cock at Derek's opening, he growled, "Are you ready?"

"Please," Derek begged, not only with his voice, but with his entire body.

Max invaded Derek's inner channel, not stopping until his whole length was buried as deep as he could get it. He froze, savouring how right this moment felt and how much he had missed the connection between them. Sinking into Derek was like coming home after a long, tiring journey.

"I dreamed about this," he whispered as he began to move.

Derek arched and shoved back, fucking himself on Max's shaft. "I dreamed of this late at night when it was just me in my hotel. I'd jerk myself off and your name would echo around the room when I came."

Bending, Max managed to brush a kiss over Derek's shoulder while he thrust in and out, dragging the head of his dick over Derek's gland with each stroke. Their panting breath filled the air along with the scent of sweat and arousal.

His balls tightened and Max slid his hand around Derek's hip to encircle the man's dick. He wanted Derek to come with him.

"Max."

Derek's whimper informed Max that his lover was close.

"Come with me, baby," he pleaded.

The first splash of wet heat over his hand threw Max into his own spine-tingling climax. He shouted as his erection swelled in Derek's passage before spilling his own cum into the only man he'd ever love.

After what felt every drop he could possibly have in his body was emptied, he and Derek collapsed into a heap on the couch. Max had just enough muscle control and mental ability to turn them, so they were wrapped in each other's arms instead of him lying on top of Derek.

"I saw you in Cheyenne for your last concert," Max confessed a few minutes later.

Derek pushed up on his elbow to stare down at Max. Frowning, he thought about that show. "I sent Yancey and the guys tickets to the concert, and I saw them there, but you weren't with them. Why didn't you come with them?"

Max shifted, his cheeks turning pink. "I got my ticket the day they went on sale. They didn't even know I went. I had to see you, but I knew I couldn't meet you face-to-face again, or else I'd probably lose what self-respect I had."

"What do you mean?" Derek climbed off the couch and headed to the table where the tray sat. He cleaned up using some napkins.

Max caught the ones he tossed at him and cleaned as well. They got dressed before wiping down the couch. Derek poured them some lukewarm coffee. They sat next to each other at the table. Max traced the rim of his cup while he thought. Derek stayed silent, hoping Max would continue to talk.

"After Denver, I told myself it would be easier without having you in front of me, where I could touch or smell you, to convince myself I'd done the right thing for both of us." Max shrugged and chuckled a little. "It's easy to delude yourself when you're avoiding pain."

"I understand, only I tend to dull my pain in other ways. Far more destructive than your method, I think." He sipped his coffee, wishing he had something to fidget with.

"It doesn't matter what we use to create an illusion of control. I knew that if I actually saw you, I would be on my knees, begging you to take me back. I would have accepted any conditions you set on our relationship, even if it meant being in the closet while we lived in Nashville." Max shoved his hand through his hair. "Yet I also know that unless I travelled with you on your tours, I'd end up second-guessing myself. So I stayed away from you in Cheyenne."

Derek reached out, covering Max's hand with his. "All those songs I sang to you and for you. Every love song is an anthem to how I feel about you. I missed you so much."

Max entwined their fingers, his grip tight and solid. "You don't have to be alone anymore. I figured something out since I saw you that last time. Even if you were still living in Nashville and still in the closet, I'd come spend all my time in there with you. I love you and I let my past dictate how my future would be spent. My mum wouldn't be proud of me for that."

"Will you come live with me on the ranch?" He could admit, if only to himself at the moment, he'd bought the ranch with the hope that someday Max would join him there.

His heart stopped beating when Max didn't respond immediately, but it returned to its normal rhythm when Max smiled and nodded.

"I'll go wherever you go, Derek, and consider myself the luckiest man in the world for the chance to love you."

His creative mind spinning, Derek shot a wild glance around the conference room. He needed a piece of paper and a pen. There was a song in that statement. Max handed him a pen and pushed a pile of napkins in his direction with an indulgent smile. Thank God he loved a man who understood him so well.

* * * *

They pulled into the long driveway, and Max studied the fences on either side of them. "What are you running?"

"Umm…about thirty head of Herefords right now, but I'm hoping you'll be interested in running the ranch. I figure you might have some ideas on what to breed and things like that. I want both our businesses to be self-supporting and successful."

"Our businesses?" Max shot a glance at Derek.

"Yes, since you've agreed to come and live with me, I'm going to make you a partner in both my music business and in the ranch. Neither of them are very much right now, but I think together we can make them into something." Derek reached over and squeezed Max's knee.

They pulled up in front of a two-storey house, built more in the old Southern plantation style than ranch style. Derek turned his SUV off and they climbed out. Max studied the building that was going to become his home.

"Who built this place?"

Derek chuckled. "The family was old money from Georgia, and they built the house as a smaller replica of the family estate. It's a little much, but we can change things as we get more comfortable here. I really picked it for the land, and one of the out-buildings was perfect for a recording studio. I have five hundred acres, and we can probably pick up more if you decide you want to expand."

Max had only brought a carry-on with him, planning on only spending one night in Austin before he flew back to Wyoming. He snatched it off the backseat then followed Derek onto the porch. He dropped it by the front door, but grabbed Derek's hand before his lover went inside.

"Show me around."

Derek did, and they held hands the entire time. None of the men and women working in the barns, on the new construction, or out around the fences looked twice at them.

"Why aren't they acting strange about us holding hands?" Max kept his voice low.

Derek smiled. "When I bought the place, I gathered everyone working here, and told them I was gay. I explained my vision for the ranch and the studio being a safe place for all kinds of people, no matter their colour, ethnicity, or sexual orientation. All of them were given an option. If they stayed, they kept their opinions to themselves without harassing anyone. If they chose to leave, I'd give them a generous parting package. Half of them left. The other half said they didn't care what we did, as long as we weren't murdering people and burying them in the back forty."

Max snapped his fingers. "Damn. That's the first thing I thought of when I saw this place."

Chuckling, Derek leaned over and kissed Max on the check. "You're a funny man. I'll give you a tour of the buildings and, tomorrow, we'll go out on horseback, so you can look at the herd and land."

"Sounds good to me."

Two hours later, standing in the bay window of Derek's house, Max waited for his boss to pick up the phone.

"Romanos." Tony's gruff voice came over the line.

"Hey, boss."

"Max, how are things in Austin?"

"You're a bastard, you know that?"

Tony chuckled. "Aren't you being a bit harsh?"

"You knew who I'd end up seeing down here. That's why you and Les sent me." He grinned.

"Of course. Derek let us know about wanting to start his own record label and studio. He told us he'd be moving to Austin. We all figured it would be a good opportunity to get you two together."

"You're worse than a bunch of matchmaking grannies," he muttered, but he wasn't able to work up too much anger towards his friends.

"We just want you to be happy, Max. Did it work?"

Footsteps sounded on the living room's hardwood floor and he turned to see Derek striding across the room, a bright smile on his face.

"I'm calling to let you know I'll be back at the ranch in two days. I'm staying long enough to pack my stuff, though I'm willing to stick around until you hire a new foreman."

"That won't be long. Brody and I have already discussed it. If you're all right with it, we think asking Tip to take over would work out."

Max thought about it. Tip was a good guy, intelligent and open-minded enough to try new things. "Sounds like a good idea to me, but can you wait until I get back before you tell him?"

"Sure. Do you need someone to pick you up at the airport?"

"Yes. Derek's flying up with me."

Derek winked as Max held out his hand to him.

"Great. Call us with the flight numbers and times. I'll make sure someone's there to pick up you up."

"Thanks, Tony. I'll call you later."

He hung up the phone and tossed it on the couch before pulling Derek into his arms. "It seems my bosses figured it was a done deal the minute I got on the plane."

"I have to admit I was certainly hoping you were a sure thing." Derek brushed a kiss over Max's cheek.

He closed his eyes and breathed in Derek's familiar scent. "Are you sure you're not doing all of this just for me? I don't want you to wake up one day and blame me for everything you gave up."

Derek pushed him far enough away to meet his gaze. "I told you this at my office. I'm doing this for me. Getting you forever is a bonus, but if you had stopped loving me, I still wouldn't regret a single decision I've made."

Max nodded, knowing he'd probably have to hear those words often until his heart accepted them.

"What will I do while you're signing artists to your label?"

"You'll be running the place. It's a working ranch with beef cattle and horses. I know you'll be able to find something to do."

Oh, he would. Max wasn't the type of guy who sat around, watching others work while he profited from their labour. He tugged Derek tight against him and they stared out of the window at the barns and pastures.

"Are we home?" he asked softly.

Max found his answer in the kiss Derek bestowed on him and in the sound of their hearts beating in time.

About the Author

There is beauty in every kind of love, so why not live a life without boundaries? Experiencing everything the world offers fascinates TA and writing about the things that make each of us unique is how she shares those insights. When not writing, TA's watching movies, reading and living life to the fullest.

T.A. Chase loves to hear from readers. You can find her contact information, website details and author profile page at http://www.total-e-bound.com.

Total-E-Bound Publishing

www.total-e-bound.com

Take a look at our exciting range of literagasmic™
erotic romance titles and discover pure quality
at Total-E-Bound.